r94

THE SPELL OF THE NORTHERN LIGHTS

Dakota
eminis-
book of
me her
f neces-

r
ts
d
si-
the

Book

North
gan to
most

D1297382

THE SPELL OF THE NORTHERN LIGHTS

Lucy Johnston Sypher

ILLUSTRATED BY
RAY ABEL

PUFFIN BOOKS

For All My Family

In this series:

The Edge of Nowhere
Cousins and Circuses
The Spell of the Northern Lights
The Turnaround Year

PUFFIN BOOKS
Published by the Penguin Group
Viking Penguin, a division of Penguin Books USA Inc.,
375 Hudson Street, New York, New York 10014, U.S.A.
Penguin Books Ltd, 27 Wrights Lane, London W8 5TZ, England
Penguin Books Australia Ltd, Ringwood, Victoria, Australia
Penguin Books Canada Ltd, 2801 John Street, Markham, Ontario, Canada L3R 1B4
Penguin Books (N.Z.) Ltd, 182–190 Wairau Road, Auckland 10, New Zealand

Penguin Books Ltd, Registered Offices: Harmondsworth, Middlesex, England

First published in the United States of America by Atheneum, 1975
Published in Puffin Books, 1991

1   3   5   7   9   10   8   6   4   2

Copyright © Lucy Johnston Sypher, 1975
All rights reserved

Library of Congress Catalog Card Number: 91-52566
ISBN 0-14-034552-3

Printed in the United States of America
Set in Janson

Contents

A Secret and a Spell	3
Scaredy-Cat	14
Magic Comes to Town	25
Stolen Gold	34
The Crystal City Picnic	45
Water Pistols	56
The Butler Baby	70
An Elevator Burns	81
Blood Poisoning	93
The Firebug	105
A One-Room School and a Cook Car	115
Four New Teachers	129
Topsy Is Sent Away	141
Second Sight at an Auction	152
The Cave Men Become Boy Scouts	164
From Now Until Christmas	174
Only Men Can Vote	183
Amory Wins the Turkey Raffle	196
The Bewitched Taffy Pull	208
Two Celebrations	221
The Snowbound Train	236
The Lucky Spell	246

A Secret
and
A Spell

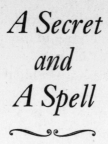

All night long the cool rain soaked the ripening North
Dakota wheatfields and softly beat on the slant roof
of the Johnstons' house, between the village of Wales
and the open prairie, right at the Edge of Nowhere.
The season was changing. From now on, August
1916 would have hot days, but many of the nights
would be chilly.

Lucy woke late the next morning and lay looking
around her room—at the tall white china pitcher in
the big basin, at the foggy mirror that always made
her red hair look faded, and at the two shelves of
her books under the eaves. Then on the chair beside
her bed she saw a shabby suitcase spilling out her rum-
pled clothes.

She jumped out of bed and shoved up the window

to check the weather. Late yesterday they had come home from their auto trip to Minneapolis, and today was her eleventh birthday. Slowly she drew in a long breath of the prairie air. Already the sun was hot, and in the garden the asters and marigolds and even the spreading pale cabbage leaves were washed clean.

Mother and Father, coming along the back walk through the garden, were talking very seriously, but it was only Father's loud rumbling voice that Lucy could hear.

"Lucy's the lucky one. These new responsibilities are just what she needs. She'll grow up fast now."

Mother murmured something, and Father continued. "Well, I wish she had more spunk. She's even afraid of the dark, I suspect."

By now they were directly under the window, so that Lucy looked down on Father's bald head and Mother's coil of dark-brown hair. Then Lucy heard Father ask a mysterious question. "Caroline, do you think we can keep this a secret from now until Christmas?"

"I doubt it," Mother replied. "Some things are hard to hide, you know. Besides, you forget that today Lucy is—" Mother glanced up and saw Lucy at the open window. "Happy Birthday, eleven times!" she called.

As Mother tilted her head back, the light glinted on her pince-nez glasses and shone on all the small lines and wrinkles of her face. To Lucy she suddenly looked old.

"Happy Birthday!" shouted Father. "And don't spend the whole day in bed. Even your slugabed brother Amory is up and gone to find Stan Sanderson and Jerry Fischer."

"And your Topsy has been scratching at the stairway door for the last hour," Mother added. "Lots of work to do, so don't put on clean clothes." And they went around to the back door.

"What's the present that's so hard to hide?" Lucy asked herself as she dug into her suitcase for her long black stockings and a dark gingham dress. Along with her clothes, out fell Clarissa, once Lucy's favorite doll, but now only a model for wardrobes Lucy designed.

"Poor Clarissa," Lucy said, as she saw that the trip in the suitcase had cracked Clarissa's china head from hair to chin. "Oh, well, now that I'm eleven, I don't suppose I'll even design you any dresses. Into the drawer you go, old girl." So Clarissa was laid away, out of sight, and Lucy felt much older.

As she dressed, Lucy thought of Father's complaint about her fears, and she resolved that from now on she'd try—really try—to have spunk and be brave.

Then Mother opened the door at the bottom of the stairs, and Topsy, Lucy's tiny tan-and-white terrier, scrambled up the bare board stairs. She dashed at Lucy, who was kneeling on the closet floor, looking for her old black button shoes.

"You're saying 'Happy Birthday,' Topsy, but let me wash my own face and find my buttonhook and then we'll eat." Topsy always understood the word *eat*, so she backed away and stood wagging her tail until they raced downstairs together.

Lucy was carrying her breakfast tray into the dining room when Amory ran in. His stiff red hair was on end, his round blue eyes were rounder than ever, and of course he was talking.

"I met Jerry on his way to mass, and he says the new priest came to Wales last night, and he's Dutch—

real Dutch, from Holland. And the new generator is here too, and pretty soon Main Street will have electricity. And all four teachers will be new—none of the old ones coming back. Three are hired, but they can't find one for seventh-eighth grade room. That's because nobody wants to teach Lucy! And Mrs. Bortz got a heart attack because both her German nephews got shot on the Western Front. And can I have two more doughnuts?"

"Can't you stop long enough to say 'Happy Birthday' to your sister?" Father asked, as Amory stuffed half a doughnut into his mouth.

Amory gulped down the chunk of doughnut. "Happy Birthday!" he shrieked. "Wait till I give you eleven wallops. You won't sit down for a week. And look, I got a present for you." From his pants pocket he pulled a water pistol.

"Oh, Amory, not a water pistol," Mother moaned.

"Needn't worry about a dry season in our backyard now," Father teased her. He turned to Amory. "I don't suppose you're giving Lucy the only water pistol you have?"

"Course not. Us three Cave Men have each got one, and now I'm giving this extra one to Lucy for her club." Amory made it sound very fair and generous, but Lucy could see the battles ahead if she accepted the pistol.

Amory, Jerry, and Stan had dug a deep pit in the backyard and called it a cave. Lucy and the three Owen girls used the little stone house nearby for their club, the Stone Age Girls. And except for the week when they had put on a circus together, the entire history of the two clubs was one of constant warfare.

"Your club's got three, and you give us only one?" Lucy shouted.

"But you girls can take turns. And we'll let you stand by the pump. How's that?" Amory smiled sweetly at her.

"You just want us girls for targets. I hate you!"

"Never saw such a pair. You'd rather squabble than celebrate," Father said sharply. Then he changed his tone. "Come open your birthday presents, Lucy. You'll never guess what you've got." Father rubbed his hands together as though he were preparing to open them himself.

On the round center table in the living room were several small packages, and on the floor was a big cardboard box. It was addressed to Miss Lucy Johnston and Miss Topsy Johnston.

"It's from all the relatives we were with in Minnesota," Mother explained.

"That box made the trip here faster than we did," Father grumbled. "Next time I'll send the whole blamed family by parcel post and skip the mudholes and the flat tires and—"

"And the hotel with bedbugs," Amory added before Mother could hush him. Then he leaned over and cut the string on Lucy's box and began pulling off the brown wrapping paper.

"It's my birthday, not yours," Lucy objected. She elbowed Amory aside, opened the box flaps, and lifted out a dog's bed, woven of varnished wicker and fitted with a green velvet mattress. On it lay clothes for Topsy to wear in her waltzing act—a doll's black satin cape and matching bonnet.

"Look, Topsy, your new costume!" Lucy shook

the cape and bonnet at Topsy, and immediately Topsy jumped, sank her sharp teeth in a crimson bonnet string, and tore it to shreds.

Lucy snatched, Topsy jerked, and the entire bonnet began to fall apart. Lucy saved it by a lucky grab. "Sometimes, Topsy, you behave like an ordinary animal and not like my miracle trick dog," Lucy scolded. Topsy put her ears way down and slunk under a rocking chair.

The first little box on the table was from Aunt Lucy, and though it was heavy, the top layers were only fuzzy cotton. But in the middle of the box was a gleaming five-dollar gold piece. Even at Father's bank Lucy had never seen a gold coin, nor had she ever before had five dollars of her own.

While Lucy stood staring at it, Amory began to plan how she could spend it. "Why don't you buy a pair of real skis? You could buy them big enough for me now, so I wouldn't have to use those barrel staves. Then later on, you'd be big enough, and I'll get bigger ones. How about that?"

Both Father and Mother laughed so hard at him that Mother took off her glasses to wipe her eyes. "Really, Amory, do you think you can sell that idea to Lucy?" she asked.

"Don't worry! He won't bamboozle me. I'm saving this gold piece for a long, long time, so I'll always have money." And Lucy carefully tucked the cotton around the beautiful coin.

"My presents for you are gold too, but they're not new," Mother said, putting two tiny packets in Lucy's hand. "I've had them since I was a girl, and now that you're eleven, they should be yours."

Mother's gifts were a gold thimble with a little

scene etched around the rim, and a gold locket decorated with raised silver flowers. A thimble, even a solid gold one, was not very exciting, but the locket Lucy had always admired. When she pried it open, she saw two small pictures, one of Mother, and one of Father.

"At Christmas, we'll get you a new chain for it. This old chain's wearing thin," Mother said as she fastened it around Lucy's neck.

Then Father handed Lucy his present. In its store paper, it looked very ordinary, but Father was so anxious for her to open it that Lucy thought it might be a joke. So she undid it very gingerly. But it wasn't a joke. It was the most exciting present of all—a box camera, loaded with a roll of film, the black number 1 showing at the round red window, ready for the first snapshot.

"Three gold presents, a box camera, and a bed for Topsy, too!" Lucy exclaimed, as she hugged Mother and then Father.

"Now to work," Father began. "Lucy, you help your mother. Amory, I'll show you where to weed." Father looked around. "Where's that boy gone?" he demanded.

"Probably out to his cave, Harry. You get him. I don't want Lucy falling in."

"So you don't care if I fall in?" Father teased. But he did go out and bellow, "Amory, come weed the garden!" When Father came back, Amory was lagging behind him.

"Have you folks forgotten this is Sunday?" Amory asked in a shocked tone. "You wouldn't want me to work on a Sunday, would you?"

"You go pull those weeds," Father barked. "Gardening on Sunday won't keep you out of heaven, though a lot of other things may."

Mother now looked closely at Amory. "All one side of your pants—soaking wet! What happened?"

"I forgot to empty that water pistol I had in my pocket. And I don't have any other old pants, do I? And if I go out all wet like this, I might catch cold, and a cold could go to pneumonia, and people do die from pneumonia, don't they?" Amory made a long, sad face.

"You go out in that garden, Amory Johnston," Father roared. "Good hot August sun will dry your pants, and if you move fast enough, you won't get pneumonia. You march!" And Amory marched.

Mother scooped several dippers of hot water from the range reservoir into the dishpan, and Lucy stood with the dish towel, ready to wipe. Then Mother left the pan, sat down on a kitchen chair, and said, "I must go lie down on the sofa. You wash the dishes, Lucy. I'm simply too tired to do them." She stood up rather shakily and went into the living room to lie down.

Mother tired at midmorning? Lucy couldn't believe her ears. She slowly washed and dried the dishes, then remembered overhearing Father speak of her "new responsibilities." She hoped doing dishes alone was not one of them.

As soon as she could, Lucy slipped out the back door with her new camera. In no time she had used a whole roll of film for snapshots of her stone clubhouse, of the flower garden, of the tallest of the five tall cottonwoods in front of their house, of the house itself, and of the wheatfield across the road—a field that stretched level and flat to the horizon, miles away.

By noon, Mother was herself again. She sent Lucy

whisking here and there—for peas from the garden, for a jar of pickles from the cellar shelves, to stir the vanilla pudding, to crush the cracker crumbs for salmon loaf.

"No birthday cake yet, Lucy," Mother said as they sat down to dinner. "Mrs. Owen is making a cake for you on Tuesday after their weekend at the Hannah church and then that wedding in Sarles." The three daughters of the Methodist minister and his wife, Gwen, Gwin, and Guinnie, were Lucy's best friends.

"How about a cake for me, too?" Amory looked up from his heaping plate. "We were on the trip when I had my twelfth birthday, so I never had a chance to blow out birthday candles. Or how about birthday candles on a pie? We boys like pie best."

"No more pies for you Cave Men!" Mother laughed. "Not after the rhubarb pie the Owens fell into when you left your cave uncovered."

"But blowing out birthday candles guarantees a lucky year," Amory argued. "How will you feel if anything bad happens to me?" His voice became mournful. "Your only son, and you won't give him a year of birthday luck."

"You're just pretending you believe. All you want is the cake," Lucy said scornfully. "You always laugh at me for being superstitious."

Father had been silently eating. Now he spoke to Mother. "I was thinking of the night Lucy was born. Janet Ross, the old Scotch nurse you had—she was a superstitious soul, wasn't she?"

"Yes, Lucy, she thought the northern lights were brilliant that night just for our new baby," Mother said, half-laughing. "When she put you in my arms, she said very seriously, 'This baby's born under the spell of the northern lights!' "

"Whatever did she mean?" Lucy was interested at once.

"Well, so much was going on that night that I have to admit," Father said, "we never even asked her."

Lucy exploded. "Do you mean my old Scotch nurse said I was born under a spell, and you never asked what the spell was?"

"Bet it was a spell to grow up dumb and homely," Amory commented.

"Stop needling your sister, Amory. And Lucy, don't you get biggety ideas," Father warned. "Don't call her 'my old Scotch nurse' as though you lived in a storybook. She was more your mother's nurse anyway—saved her life, as well as yours."

"I wish I could have had Janet Ross every time I had a baby," Mother said wistfully. "Maybe she could have saved the others, too." Lucy knew that Mother had lost three babies, all born too early, and each time Mother herself had nearly died.

"Couldn't we write Miss Ross somewhere?" Lucy asked. "Here I am going around with a spell on me and nobody bothered to ask what it was. Who knows —why, I might turn into a—"

"Toad!" yelled Amory, and then put a heaping spoonful of vanilla pudding into his mouth, as though he hadn't said a word.

"She was visiting Mrs. Stewart in Langdon— they're cousins. And she went home to Scotland soon after you were born. We could ask Dr. Stewart for her address," Mother said.

"And what should we write?" Father began to tease. "Should we begin with 'How are you?' And then go on to 'Please reply posthaste and tell what the spell is on our daughter.' " He shook his head. "Sounds as though we lived in the Middle Ages instead of 1916."

"Northern lights couldn't put a spell on anyone," Amory growled.

"Some people believe the stars control their lives, so why not the northern lights?" By now Lucy was convinced. "They're in the sky too, and they're bright—brighter some years than others."

"They're nothing by themselves." Amory belittled them. "Sunspots cause them. So how could they cast a spell? And who believes in spells anyway?"

"One thing Miss Ross did say, Lucy, was that we'd chosen the perfect name for a baby born when the lights were so brilliant," Father went on.

"Of course. *Lucy* means *light*, doesn't it?"

"Yes, and you can be thankful she was content with that and didn't want you named for the northern lights. You'd have been Aurora Borealis Johnston."

"Wait till I tell the boys!" and Amory ran out the back door, chanting, "Lucy, the roaring, boring Johnston, my roaring boring sister!"

Scaredy-Cat

That night Lucy was falling asleep, thinking of her mysterious spell, when Father whispered at her bedroom door, "Lucy, Lucy, get up and see the northern lights. They're as bright as the night you were born."

Lucy rolled out of bed, pulled on her shoes, and tiptoed down the stairs after Father, who carried a kerosene lamp. In the kitchen he held out her coat, helped her find the sleeves and then the buttons.

He was still whispering to her, when she asked, out loud, "Why just us?"

"Shhhh!" He put his finger to his lips. "Your mother is sound asleep, and she's very tired. And Amory only grunted when I invited him to get up. We could see the lights from this north window," he continued, "but I want you to see the entire sweep across the sky."

Silently they went through the back shed, and Father closed the outside door so that it made not a sound. Lucy's first feeling was a shivery chill. Out in the backyard, Father stopped. There before her and over her head glowed the strange rays of light, shifting and flickering, illuminating the whole wide prairie sky.

"They're putting on a show for your birthday," Father announced. "I didn't want you to miss it."

Of course Lucy had seen northern lights many times, but this was the most dazzling display ever. Not just white, but yellow and golden and in some places even red.

"Other nights, when I'm asleep, are they like this?" she asked.

"No, these are unusual. Amory's right about sunspots causing the northern lights. So every eleven years, when there has been a burst of spots on the sun, the northern lights are especially bright."

Lucy stared up at the radiant sky. "They have such a powerful, magical look—can't you believe they might put a spell on a baby born when they're at their brightest?" Since Father said nothing, Lucy went on. "If they change every eleven years, maybe the spell began when I was born. And now eleven years are over, and so's the spell. I wonder if I'll be different now."

"That's a good idea," Father agreed. "It could have been a spell that made you afraid of so many things." He looked down at her and said very seriously, "Someday you've got to outgrow all those fears and have more courage."

This was an echo of what she'd overheard from her window, but she didn't ask questions. She was thinking of all the fears her folks didn't know she had. She did fear being alone in the dark and she was still afraid to take responsibility for anything important, although when she had to, it seemed to go all right.

But she never told anyone that she was also afraid of big dogs, of burglars, of blood and wounds, and of war coming to her country. She had a fear of any strangers and of a fire that might burn their house. And most of all, she feared Mother or Father might die. That was the worst.

Father turned to go indoors. "If your eleven-year enchantment is over, watch out. You may change entirely, like Cinderella. Remember how she got out of the kitchen, forever?"

"I hope my change isn't *into* the kitchen. Today I've washed dishes for hours," Lucy complained.

Father grinned at her. "Something has changed then, hasn't it?" And together they tiptoed into the house.

The next morning, while Mother again lay on the sofa, Lucy did the breakfast dishes, swept the middle of the kitchen floor, and gave a swipe with a dust-cloth to Mother's piano and the mahogany bookcase. She was about to escape outdoors when the phone rang.

Lucy stood on tiptoe to take the receiver off the high wall phone and shouted "Hello!" into the cupped mouthpiece.

"Oh, it's you, Lucy," Father said. "Is Amory there?"

"No, he's gopher-hunting with Jerry," Lucy explained.

"This once, then, you can go in his place. Ed the butcher has some pork chops for our dinner. Tell your mother it's all right. I saw Ed only a few minutes ago, and he's sober."

Lucy had never gone to the butcher shop alone, for Ed the butcher was often drunk. One day when she was very small, she had been in the shop with Mother when suddenly Mother grabbed her arm and fled to the bank. There Father had left his desk and gone himself to collect their roast beef.

Now Father was waiting at the other end of the line for her answer. "Lucy, you still there?" he asked impatiently.

"Yes, I'm here," she breathed faintly into the phone.

"Then hurry along, before he sells them to someone else. And one thing more, Lucy. Don't take Topsy out of the yard. I hear there's an epidemic of distemper. The young dogs are all dying from it—there's no cure, you know." And he hung up.

"What is it, dear?" Mother asked.

"He wants me to get pork chops at the butcher shop," Lucy said unhappily.

"Splendid! We'll have them for dinner this noon." Then seeing Lucy hesitate, Mother spoke sharply. "Your father wouldn't send you unless he was sure the butcher is sober. Don't be such a scaredy-cat."

Lucy walked the four blocks to Main Street at a snail's pace. At the butcher shop, she first looked in the open door and saw the butcher standing with his back to her. Only after she was inside and near the counter did she see what he was doing. His head was tipped far back, and he was drinking from a flat bottle.

She started to back out, but it was too late. He turned and saw her.

"I thought your brother was coming," he said crossly. "You aren't your brother, are you?"

"No, sir," answered Lucy in a shaky voice. "My father sent me instead—for the chops."

"Got them right here. Only have to chop them off," he said, fumbling with the refrigerator door and then pulling it open. He reached in and took out a long piece of pork. Then lifting a great cleaver from the hook on the side of his chopping block, he stared straight at her. "Chops have to be chopped. You know that much, don't you?"

"Yes, sir," Lucy replied, her eyes intent on the wide, sharp cleaver in his hairy red hand.

He began hacking off the chops with tremendous bangs, counting out loud. "One, two, three, four," and when he got to fourteen, he stood with the cleaver

poised over the pork and asked, "How many does your mother want?"

"I think Mother usually gets only eight or ten," Lucy answered mildly.

"Today she'll get what I give her," he said scowling. And he went on chop, chop, chopping. The piece of pork grew shorter and shorter, and the pile of chops grew higher and higher. Lucy foresaw days and days of pork chop dinners, but she didn't dare to argue.

He might have gone on chopping all the meat in sight if he hadn't been interrupted. On the wall of his shop hung a magnificent cuckoo clock. Its gilded pendulums never stopped swinging, and the white hands and numbers on its brown wooden face always showed the right time. Every hour, on the hour, the small double doors at the top opened and a bright yellow cuckoo bobbed out to say the proper number of *cuckoo*s.

Now as the clock whirred, Lucy looked up at it. The cuckoo popped out and cheerily called eleven *cuckoo*s. Ed the butcher stopped chopping, listened until the last *cuckoo*, and then put the cleaver back on its hook, jerked a long stretch of paper from the roller on the counter, and threw the heap of chops on it. Clumsily he pushed the paper over them and wound yards and yards of string around the package.

Leaning way over the counter, he shoved the bundle toward her, and Lucy saw that he had big tears in his eyes. She wanted to grab the chops and run, but he had begun to talk to her.

"That was my father's clock from Germany. Used to hang in our big shop in Chicago." His tears began to run down his cheeks into his long, drooping moustache. "And now—look where I am. Selling chops in a hick village that doesn't know tripe from T-bone." He began to sob.

Lucy picked up the awkward bundle. She felt she should say something, but she didn't know tripe from T-bone either. So she only said, "Thank you for the chops. Charge them, please."

She started for the door, but looking over her shoulder, she saw him lurch around the corner and come toward her. She speeded up. Behind her she heard his slow, heavy footsteps. Out the open door she flew. But when she looked back, she understood. The butcher wasn't chasing her. He was shutting the shop door, closing up for the rest of the day.

Loaded with the bulky package, she couldn't easily run home. So she walked along, deciding what she should tell Mother. If she told about seeing Ed drink from a bottle when she went in, Mother would be cross that she had gone in at all. But if she didn't tell about his being drunk, how could she explain the mountain of pork chops?

Rounding the corner by the Catholic priest's house, she remembered the new priest—"real Dutch—from Holland." So she walked even more slowly past the high picket fence.

It was then that she heard the strange voice for the first time. "Faa-ther!" croaked the harsh voice from the other side of the fence. "Faa-ther! Faa-ther!" it rasped again, like a gargle in a dry, scratchy throat.

Lucy stopped, stood as high as she could, and craned her neck to see over the fence. She found herself staring directly into the face of a smiling, gray-haired man, who was leaning over to pull up tiny carrots.

"Good morning," he said gently, as he straightened up and brushed some dirt from his dark suit. "I'm Father Van Mert, the new priest."

"I'm Lucy Johnston," she replied. "Good morning, Mr. Van Mert—I mean Reverend Van Mert—I mean Father."

And from low on the ground between the tall rows of corn, the grating voice repeated her last word. "Faa-ther!" Yet the only person in sight was the new priest, who now turned toward the house, waved his handful of carrots at Lucy, and went in.

The rest of the way, Lucy forgot about the butcher and puzzled over that spooky voice, not like anything she'd ever heard before.

Suddenly she was at her own back gate, and Rip, the Torsens' bad-tempered police dog, was rushing at her. Probably he was out for pork chops and not for her, but Lucy feared Rip as she would a wild animal.

She started to run. Rip gave a leap for the chops, almost knocking her over. She snatched the bundle back from him so fast that he was left with only a piece of paper dangling from his mouth. With her heart beating hard, Lucy reached for the latch on the gate. She was just about to open it wide when she remembered Father's warning about distemper.

She knew that the germs passed from dog to dog. If she let Rip into their yard, Topsy might catch distemper and die. Her fear for Topsy became greater than her fear of Rip. Instead of opening the gate, she faced him.

"You go home, Rip!" she commanded in her loudest voice. Rip backed away, his eyes still fixed on the meat package. "Get going!" Lucy yelled, stamping her foot. But Rip started for her again, looking very fierce.

He looked so wolfish that Lucy remembered a story about people who saved themselves from hungry wolves by throwing away their food. Quickly she pulled a single chop from the torn paper and threw it as far as she could. Rip took off after the chop, Lucy opened the gate, hurried through, and clicked it shut.

Once inside her own yard, she felt rather proud of herself. So much for Rip Torsen.

Mother was waiting for her in the kitchen. "What on earth kept you so long?" she asked. Then she noticed the torn wrappings. "And what on earth happened to the meat?"

"The Torsens' Rip tried to get it."

Mother took the big bundle, hefted it, and exclaimed, "Good heavens, Lucy, did you buy a whole pig?"

"The butcher wouldn't listen to me when I said how many you wanted. He told me you'd get—" Lucy stopped. If she repeated what the butcher had said, there'd be trouble. "Can we ever eat this many?" Lucy worried.

"Oh, yes," Mother assured her. "With Amory around, consuming a whole hog is easy."

"And I've got to tell you, Mother, about a scary voice I heard. It came from under the corn in the priest's garden, and it croaked 'Faa-ther!' It gave me the shivers."

"Nonsense, Lucy. You get shivers too easily. Don't forget you're eleven years old now. Go ahead and set the table, while I cook these." Mother put chop after chop to sizzle in the two black frying pans on the coal range.

"Hurry," Mother called over the sputter of the cooking. "It's almost time for your father."

"Faa-ther!" Lucy echoed raspingly, but she couldn't sound like that croak in the priest's garden. Did anybody ever speak like that, or was it only a voice and not a person, Lucy wondered.

Magic Comes to Town

Soon Father came in. "Caroline, the strangest thing just happened to me," he began as he came through the door.

"I suppose you heard a voice calling 'Faa-ther!' to you. And did it scare you the way it did Lucy?" Mother joked.

"Did Lucy hear it, too?" Father asked. "I was passing the priest's garden when I heard someone calling to me, 'Faa-ther! Faa-ther!' But when I looked around, no one was there, only a crow strutting along behind me. Uncanny, that's what it was."

"The corn talks to Lucy, and a crow talks to you. What a pair!" Mother brushed past them, carrying the big platter of chops into the dining room. "Bring the mashed potatoes and the beet greens, Lucy. Probably you're both hungry. That's what's wrong."

They had just sat down to eat when the phone rang. Lucy answered. It was Gwin Owen. "We're home from Hannah, but we've got to go now for Papa to marry those people in Sarles, and you'll never guess what Papa heard a few minutes ago when he was walking at the back of our garden, where it's right next to the Catholic churchyard. He heard a—"

"I know what he heard," Lucy broke in. "It was a voice croaking 'Faa-ther! Faa-ther!' wasn't it?"

"That's true," Gwin admitted in surprise. "But we all call him Papa, so who would call him Father? And how did you know, anyway?"

"I heard the voice first, and now my father thinks a bird talked to him. I'll tell you about it tomorrow. We're eating now," and Lucy hung up.

Back at the table, Lucy began to think out loud. "In French history, Joan of Arc heard voices when she was a little girl, didn't she?" Lucy said dreamily. "And wasn't there a saint that talked with birds?"

"You're not Joan of Arc, Lucy," Mother said firmly. "And your father's a good man, but he's no saint. Now eat your dinner while it's hot."

For a minute they ate quietly. Lucy passed a bit of pork to Topsy, who always sat during meals at Lucy's feet, hidden by the big white tablecloth.

Mother poured Father's tea into a plain white china cup and set it on a yellow saucer with a green rim. "Look, we've broken so many handles off the cups that nothing matches," she said. "When I have the Ladies Aid here next week, they'll have to bring their own cups unless I can buy some new ones before then." She passed the mismatched cup and saucer to Father and went on.

"We've never been to Crystal City, across the border, but I hear it has a good china shop. If you could get away from the bank for a whole day, we could buy china and have Amory's birthday picnic on the Pembina River, too."

"Goodness, Caroline, what a gadabout you are!" Then Father asked anxiously, "Do you feel up to having the Ladies Aid here next week?"

"Yes, they bring their own cakes, and I'm furnishing only the coffee and the dishes, and the house, too, of course. At this season all the other women are busier than I am, so it's good for me to do it now and get it over with. You know that."

"If that's what you want, I suppose it's all right. And with Lucy older, she'll be a big help."

Lucy winced at the words "a big help," but she felt better when Father added, "How about my paying Lucy and each of the Owen girls to help you get ready for this shindig? Perhaps a dime each for a morning's housework?" To Lucy, this was real wages.

The screen door slammed, and Amory burst in, shouting, "Do you know what the new priest brought to town?"

"Go wash in the kitchen before you sit down," Father ordered.

"Straight from gophers to the table. What are you thinking of?" Mother scolded.

"Both of you children wash your hands twice as much as usual for the next few weeks," Father said seriously. "Infantile paralysis is spreading around the county. Soap and water may not help, but it won't do you any harm either."

While Amory banged the kitchen basin from its hook and swished his hands in warm water from the reservoir, Mother spoke. "Infantile paralysis always makes me tremble. No one can tell when it may strike us. Is it near Wales yet?"

"So far, it's south of Langdon, I hear. But, of course, you're right. Until the first frost—a real deep freeze —any child can pick it up." Then he added   a comforting way, "I wouldn't worry. Our children have been lucky every fall."

Amory came back to the table and started to talk where he'd begun. "Well, do you folks know what the new priest brought to town?" Amory never paused for answers to his questions.

"Jerry went to early mass, and afterward the priest showed him his pet crow and it talks, and its name is Magic, because the farmer that gave it to him said it must have stayed alive by magic after a dog broke its wing, and it still can't fly very well."

"So a bird did talk to me!" Father laughed and shook his finger at Mother.

"Couldn't we get a crow?" Amory asked. "Wouldn't you like a crow to say 'Faa-ther!' to you? Jerry says it talks clear as anything."

"One crow talking to me is quite enough! Your mother has already called me a liar about that one."

"You have to slit its tongue before it can talk, don't you?" Amory continued.

"That's only a cruel myth," Father answered. "Lucy, hand me the bird book on the middle shelf." He pointed to one of the six bookcases lining the walls of the room. Then he found the page about crows. "This says that tame crows do imitate people, but only because they're very bright. I never knew crows were that smart. Sometimes they say several words."

"Does this crow say more than 'Faa-ther'?" Lucy asked Amory.

"Jerry says it won't even try another word, and it says that one only to Father Van Mert."

"You're wrong there, Amory. It spoke to me and to Mr. Owen." Father paused. "Come to think of it, both of us wear black suits. Your mother insists I'm no saint, but that crow may think I'm a priest."

"Imagine a talking crow coming to live in Wales, North Dakota," Mother said, as though she still didn't believe it.

"And a new priest, too, don't forget," Father said. "I should call on him this evening. Want to come with me, children, and meet the magic bird?"

"No, I'm going with Jerry tomorrow," Amory said.

"I'll go, if I don't have to touch it," Lucy replied. "You know feathers give me the creeps."

"Yes, and that's my fault," Father said. "I should never have let Mrs. Scheler hand you that fluttering baby chicken when you were so small. Scared the wits out of you."

"No wits, that's Lucy's problem. Afraid of birds!" Amory jeered.

"I'm not afraid of birds. I just can't touch feathers."

"And I wish some magic could cure you of that," Father added. Then he spoke to Mother. "You wanted to go to the post office? I'm taking the auto so I can see some farmers out in the country. I'll drop you off on the way."

"If you're going out to farms, Harry, don't wear that good new suit," Mother warned.

So Father went upstairs to change, and in a few

minutes both Father and Mother drove off in their black Regal automobile.

Soon after, Amory disappeared upstairs. When he came down, he was wearing Father's new black suit. The trousers were rolled in great lumps above his heels, and the sleeves were rolled in great lumps above his hands.

"Who said you could wear that!" Lucy exclaimed.

"Don't you tattle," Amory said. "I'm going to see if Magic will talk to me if I wear a black suit."

"Wait, I want to come, too." And Lucy followed him out.

Together they ran along the walk to the priest's garden, Amory yanking up the trousers every few steps to keep from falling. Then, while Lucy watched from across the road, he stuck out his chest and walked importantly beside the picket fence.

Nothing happened. So he walked past a second time, flapping a coat sleeve to attract the crow's attention. Again nothing happened.

The third time he walked by, he flapped the whole coat. And a whole lot happened. Magic cawed from the garden, "*Caw, caw, caw!*" Amory tripped over the long trousers and fell flat on his face, and Mother came around the corner.

"Amory, what are you doing in your father's best suit?" Mother screeched almost as loud as Magic. "Look! You've torn a hole in one knee."

"And that stupid old bird didn't say 'Faa-ther!' to me, not even once," Amory said in disgust.

"Well, your own father will say something to you tonight," Mother scolded. "And it won't sound like magic, either."

"Anyway," Amory said to Lucy as they walked

along behind Mother, "someday I'll be a father, and then Magic will talk to me. But Magic won't ever talk to you, Lucy, because you'll never be a father, never!"

And for that, Lucy had no answer.

Early that evening Father and Lucy walked to the priest's house. When Father knocked on the front door, the priest came out, and he recognized Lucy at once. He even remembered her name.

"Good evening, Lucy," he said. "And this must be your father, Mr. Johnston." He held out his hand to each of them in turn. "Let's sit here on the porch. My house is filled with packing cases now," and he brought out three chairs.

"I came by to welcome you," Father began. "If there's anything I can do, let me know. We're not Catholics, but in a village this small, everybody helps everybody else."

Lucy had noticed that Father Van Mert had deep laugh lines around his eyes, so she wasn't surprised to hear him joke in reply. "Yes, I had one man here before noon today, and he used the same words. 'Everybody here helps everybody else, and could you lend me a couple of dollars?'"

Father burst out laughing. "I'll wager that was old man Butler, wasn't it? But I have to admit I give him a dollar now and then myself. He's not a drinker, and those ten children have to eat, even if the old man doesn't work."

Before long, Father Van Mert was telling them about his life in Holland and about his coming to Dakota, first as a missionary and then staying as a parish priest.

"When I write home about the bitter winters and the hot summers and the winds and the flat, empty miles, my folks don't understand why I want to live here. But I like it. This land has laid a spell on me, I think."

Lucy pricked up her ears. A priest with a spell on him? And Father winked slyly at her before he answered the priest. "I understand. My relatives think I'm mad not to go back to teach at the university again, but I like this prairie much better than the city. Maybe this land does put spells on some people."

Before they left, Father asked, "Is that talking crow in bed, or could we meet him?"

"He's on the back porch in his big cage," explained the priest, as he led them there. "The cage is to protect him from a dog or a cat. He can fly only a few feet and then not very high. So he's a sitting—well, not a sitting duck but a sitting crow, if he's attacked."

When Father Van Mert opened the cage, he talked softly to the crow until Magic croaked twice, "Faa-ther! Faa-ther!" Next the priest asked Lucy, "Should I get him out so you can hold him a minute?"

"Oh, no, no," Lucy answered very positively, "I like him best inside his cage." And she backed away so hurriedly she almost fell off the porch.

"Lucy is fascinated by Magic's talents, but she prefers all birds at a distance," Father said, and Lucy nodded, rather violently.

When they were leaving, Father Van Mert asked, "What time can I pick up mail tomorrow at the post office?"

"Perhaps by three o'clock," Father told him. "But because we're next to the last town on the Hannah branch line, the train is often very late."

"Mail's important to me now—the war, and all my folks are in Holland. Ever since Germany took Belgium two years ago, I fear for them. I pray for them, but my fears are great."

"I understand." That was all Father said, but he looked gloomy.

Walking home, Lucy remarked, "Even when he's a priest, he's got fears, hasn't he?"

"Of course he has. But his fear is what I'd call a sensible fear."

"You mean my fear of touching Magic isn't very sensible, don't you?"

"Something like that," Father said, and smiled down at her. "But now that your spell is changing, I can see you becoming brave as a lion."

"Well, I hope I won't be like the Cowardly Lion in the *Wizard of Oz*," Lucy replied, for she knew she wasn't about to touch Magic, much as she liked the sound of his name.

Stolen Gold

"Why not take the Dickermans the presents you bought them on the trip?" Mother suggested the next morning. "And pick some flowers for Mrs. Dickerman. I'm going to rest until time to get dinner."

So in a few minutes Lucy was on the dusty road around the block, carrying a big handful of asters and larkspur and the four packages—a foot-long pencil each for Rudolph and Adolph, the twins who would soon start first grade; a barrette for nine-year-old Hilda; and a celluloid rattle for Baby Charlie, who was only six weeks old.

In the front yard, Mrs. Dickerman was putting Charlie in a wicker baby carriage. "Oh, flowers from your mother," Mrs. Dickerman said. "You've been home two days, and I haven't seen her out."

"No, she's still awfully tired from the trip," Lucy explained, but as she said this, she wondered again whether Mother wasn't sick, instead of tired.

"Look how big our Charlie is, and only a seven-month baby, and now—fat!"

Lucy peered over the carriage. Charlie wasn't only fat, he had golden hair and little doll-like hands. "Why, he's beautiful," Lucy said.

"Yah, he is. And he's the only one home now. The twins and my Hilda are out at their Aunt Aggie's. No infantile out there." Lucy said nothing, because she remembered hearing they had lost a little boy from that, before they moved to town.

"And I bought this carriage from Mrs. Flint. Just like new, isn't it?"

"Mrs. Flint keeps everything like new," Lucy agreed. "My father says she even keeps her Morrie and Dorrie like new."

"She came from St. Paul. That's why she's different, not like us. Now I got to take a pie out of the oven. Want to wheel Charlie over to show him to your ma?"

Lucy didn't wait. She whisked the carriage out the gate and wheeled it rapidly along the bumpy road. At her own front gate, she called, "Mother, do come see Charlie. I'm taking him for his first ride in the Flints' baby carriage. He's grown!"

Mother came out the door. "And only six weeks ago, we thought he couldn't live." Mother leaned over the carriage, where Baby Charlie lay staring up at both of them.

"Wouldn't you love to have a baby? A girl, of course, and as beautiful as Charlie," Lucy said very definitely.

"Not everybody can have babies as handsome as the Dickerman children. We can't compete. You had a big mouth and not a spear of hair." Mother made her sound like a cartoon.

Charlie now wriggled a little, opened his mouth, and let out a full-scale yell. " 'Bye, Mother, I'm taking him home." Lucy backed the carriage around, headed for the road, and pushed at full speed, while Charlie screamed.

As she went tearing along the road, Lucy was of two minds about babies. A pretty little baby girl to dress up and take for a quiet ride in her carriage would be fun, but a screamer would be a bore. "A roaring boring baby," Lucy said to herself.

When she delivered Charlie to his mother, Mrs. Dickerman at once undid the top of her dress, picked up Charlie and began to feed him. He stopped crying instantly, and Lucy felt that mothers had an unfair advantage.

"I'll take the presents out to the kids," Mrs. Dickerman called as Lucy left. "They're not coming into town until school. Kids catch infantile in towns."

By three in the afternoon, Lucy and Mother were on their way to the parsonage, Lucy in her best blue-and-white plaid dress and her patent leather shoes, and Mother in her blue voile, looking a little blue in the face too, Lucy noticed.

To show her presents, Lucy wore her gold locket, had her gold thimble in her sewing basket, and carried her camera to snap pictures of everyone. The five-dollar gold piece she left at home, hidden under her pillow.

The parsonage was a very small house next to the Methodist church. The yard was back to back with the land surrounding the Catholic church, and luckily it was a large backyard for a large garden. The minister's salary was so small that a big garden was needed to feed the family of six.

At their front gate the three Owens girls and six-year-old Edward sang "*Happy birthday to you,*" as they swung open the gate. Edward insisted upon swatting Lucy eleven times on the backside, and then the three girls led her and Mother into the house. There Mrs. Owen was lighting the candles on a round pink cake in the middle of the dining-room table.

Mrs. Owen was almost pretty, but she always looked worn out from all the sewing, cooking, canning, gardening, and church work that filled her days. "Our Edward wanted the candles lit right away," she explained, smiling. "He keeps thinking it's his birthday."

"Lucy," Gwin began to talk at once, "you should know right away that you must call Guinnie by her full name now—Guinevere. Great-aunt Maud Guinevere doesn't like that nickname for her namesake, does she, Guinnie—no, I mean Guinevere?"

This shift in names startled Lucy. She had never paid much attention to Guinnie, the youngest of the girls and not yet nine, but she could see that calling her Guinevere somehow put her higher on the family ladder. "Can I still call you Gwen and Gwin?" Lucy asked.

"Of course," Gwin assured her. "We aren't going to get Great-aunt Maud Guinevere's money, are we, Mother?"

Mrs. Owen said a mild "Shhhh," as though *money* were a swear word, but Guinnie-Guinevere looked quite smug.

"Time to blow out the candles," announced Edward.

"We just lit them. Wait," begged Gwen.

Edward never listened to anyone. He leaned over the cake. "Hurry up, Lucy, or I'll blow first and I'll get the wish."

"Shall I? So soon?" Lucy asked, looking around and seeing they weren't going to stop their darling Edward.

And when she saw his cheeks puff out for a powerful blow, Lucy drew in a mighty breath. She had no time to concoct a perfect wish for the year ahead, so she quickly skimmed one idea from the top of her mind.

"This year may I be brave!" she wished. And then she blew, a tremendous, breathy blow.

All the candles went out at once. But glancing at Edward, Lucy saw that he had blown at the same instant. That brat! Had he spoiled her wish?

Edward was already yelling, "I blew them out! I'll get the wish!"

"But it's Lucy's birthday, my love," Mrs. Owen said patiently. "Now Lucy will cut the cake and get her presents."

"What do I get?" Edward, in his white ruffled shirt and his velvet pants, climbed on a chair and grabbed for the tissue-wrapped presents.

For once, all three Owen girls shouted, "No, Edward!" And he was so astonished that he got down.

Then Lucy cut the cake, and while they sat around the table eating the cake and the two mothers drinking tea, Lucy opened the packages at her place. Mrs. Owen had embroidered a yellow apron for her, and Gwen gave her the book *Anne of Green Gables*, which she said every girl in Canada knew by heart.

Next Edward handed her a box with eleven glass marbles. Lucy thought they were beautiful, but within moments Edward said, "Now give them back. They're not yours to keep. They're mine." And though his three sisters giggled at him, Lucy handed them back with a frown.

Because Gwin was devoted to Topsy, she had wrapped a little brown-and-white china dog for Lucy and a bone for Topsy in the same packet. And Guinevere's gift was a silver spoon, with the heads of King George and Queen Mary carved on the handle. Lucy was impressed.

"When we were back East visiting Great-aunt Maud, she sent you this," explained Guinevere. "It's their Majesties on the handle, you know."

"Their Majesties," Lucy repeated out loud. She loved the word. Not Wales, not North Dakota, not the whole United States had anything so romantic.

"You call your papa now, Edward. It's time for his present." Then to Mother, Mrs. Owen went on. "Every afternoon when Mr. Owen gets the paper, the news is so awful that he works on his model trains in the cellar more than ever—to forget."

"I know," Mother said. "In this Battle of the Somme men are dying by thousands and thousands every day." Mother paused. "But in Canada on your visit, you must have felt close to the tragic slaughter."

Mrs. Owen looked about to cry. "Family after family—young men, some already young fathers, going in shiploads to France to—" She must have noticed the girls' sad faces, for she abruptly shifted. "Here's Mr. Owen with his present for you, Lucy."

Mr. Owen, a small, serious man, came in, holding

something behind his back. "Happy Birthday, Lucy," he said solemnly.

"Thank you," Lucy answered very formally. She was shy with Mr. Owen.

"I haven't wrapped it, but here it is," and he held out a small bright-red wooden box with a hinged cover and a hasp to hold it shut. "You're almost like one of our girls, so I made it for you." And he smiled.

Lucy was overwhelmed, not so much by the box, fine as that was, as by his having made it just for her. She'd never dreamed he could be so nice.

"Look inside!" Gwin told her.

Lucy opened the box and saw that inside the cover he had carved LUCY'S TREASURE BOX. And in the box was a small red padlock with its own brass key.

For a moment she held the box, thinking of how much time he must have spent making it so perfect. "Mr. Owen, how ever did you know that I need a box with a lock right now to hold my gold presents, especially my gold coin?"

Mr. Owen continued to smile at her. "It's not store-bought. It's better. I'm glad you like it." He spoke with Mother a few minutes and then disappeared into his cellar again.

Soon Mother left to fix supper, and Mrs. Owen suggested everyone go outside while she picked up the dining room.

Out in the front yard, Lucy lined them up for a snapshot, but when she clicked the camera, Edward stuck out his tongue. She had only one more chance on that film, but this time Edward pinched Gwin, who let out a screech that made both Gwen and Guinevere turn their heads.

After that, no one knew what to do to fill the next

hour, but Edward, as usual, decided it. "Let's play hide the thimble and use Lucy's solid gold one."

"All right, but let's use any old thimble and not my gold one," Lucy said.

"You're a selfish pig, that's what you are!" Edward taunted. And he snatched the thimble from her open sewing basket before she could stop him.

"It's safe, Lucy. We won't go out of the yard," Gwen assured her.

"It's much more like finding treasure if the thimble's gold," Guinevere said.

"Besides, I'll cry if you don't let me use your gold one," Edward threatened. And since no one ever crossed Edward, Lucy couldn't refuse.

"My turn first, and I'll go around the church and hide it there," Edward said. He ran off, they counted to fifty very slowly, and he called, "Come on. Bet you can't find it!"

Immediately they went to the far side of the church, and they poked at every hummock of grass, looked under every weed, and examined even the chinks between the lower concrete blocks. Edward stayed beside them the whole time, grinning slyly.

At last the girls gave up. "You win, Edward," Lucy granted. "Show us where it is."

"I'm smarter than all you Stone Age Girls," Edward gloated. "I just said I hid it here to fool you. It's on that big flat stone at the back of our garden."

For a minister's boy, this seemed dishonest, but Lucy held her tongue, and they all trooped to the one big flat stone next to the Catholic church property.

In a second they saw there was no thimble there. "It's gone!" Edward exclaimed. "Who took it?" He did look surprised, but Lucy didn't trust Edward.

"Hand it over, Edward. It's worth a lot of money, and it's mine." Lucy went toward him with her hand out.

"I left it on that stone. Somebody stole it." He began to sob. Gwen scolded him, gently. Gwin threatened to tattle. And Guinevere argued that he'd look silly with a thimble. But Edward only wept, and between sniffling sobs, he insisted, "I haven't got it. Somebody came in the yard and stole it."

Lucy was not convinced, but his sisters were, so Lucy gave up. "By tomorrow it'll be back on the stone, and you bring it over to my house, Edward. Please?"

"We'll find it for you," Gwen promised. "We won't tell Mama and Papa now. Poor Edward would be so upset."

"Upset! What about me?" Lucy wanted to say. But instead she made the best of it. "You know I loved it because it used to be Mother's and it's pure gold, but I can't sew with a thimble, anyway."

Gwen walked home with her, and to keep from talking about the missing thimble, Lucy told about her spell. "Did you ever know anybody in Canada born under the spell of the northern lights? When I was born, my old Scotch nurse said I was."

"What does it do to you? Why didn't you ever tell me before?" Gwen asked in a rush.

"My folks told me on my birthday, and we don't any of us know what it is. My mother's going to write to Scotland to ask the nurse." Lucy watched Gwen's face. Obviously even Canada hadn't prepared Gwen for a friend born under a spell.

"Is it a secret? Don't you feel special? Can't you

guess what it might be? A spell! Anything might happen to you."

"Amory knows about it, so it's not exactly secret," Lucy admitted. "Northern lights change every eleven years, so my spell might be over, or changing, and it could have been—" Lucy hated to have Gwen think her a scaredy-cat, so she now asked a question. "Gwen, you're twelve, and are you still afraid of being alone in the dark?"

Gwen answered immediately. "I wouldn't tell anybody but you. Even when I know it can't be true, I always think somebody's breathing right behind me in the dark. I'm scared stiff."

"I am too!" Lucy was comforted. "Tomorrow I'll be over, and we'll search some more for the thimble," she said as they parted.

At home it was suppertime, so Lucy didn't have to report her lost birthday gift. At the table she bragged to Amory, "Mr. Owen made me a box with a padlock. It's safe as the bank vault." When Amory only went on eating his lemon pie, Lucy said what she had meant to tell no one.

"I'm putting my five-dollar gold piece in that box, and I'm locking it tight, and I'm hiding the key, and the smartest burglar in the state couldn't steal it."

"Phooey on your little ten-cent padlock!" Amory was ready to argue. "I'll bet anybody could steal from—"

Mother interrupted. "Can't we have one meal without an argument?" she asked, wearily.

Father, who had been thinking of something else, now boomed. "Don't let me hear of your trying to break that padlock, Amory."

"I didn't say I'd break it. I just said—" Amory looked at Father's clenched jaw, and he didn't finish his sentence.

The last few minutes of the meal were very silent.

The
Crystal City
Picnic

～๑๑～

"Lucy, get up. We're leaving soon for Crystal City,"
Mother called upstairs early on Wednesday. When
Lucy was dressed and downstairs, she saw Father in
the backyard checking the tires and Amory packing
his fishing tackle. Mother looked so much better this
morning that Lucy asked whether she was all well.

"Perhaps not permanently well, but maybe it takes
a trip to cure a trip," Mother answered.

"Crystal City," Lucy said slowly, as she sloshed
milk on her lukewarm oatmeal. "Such a lovely name
for a town. It must be beautiful. I can hardly wait
to get there. Is that giant-sized chocolate cake
Amory's?"

"Yes, the poor boy didn't have one. The chocolate frosting is thick enough to make us all sick, but

that's what he ordered."

"Mmmmm—it's good!" Lucy slipped her little finger around the bottom of the cake and collected a blob of frosting.

"I forgot to buy him candles," Mother confessed. "Maybe he won't notice. Now help me pack. The cake goes in this big cardboard box, and the rest into our new picnic suitcase."

The suitcase was fitted with enamel cups and plates and had little straps inside the cover for knives, forks, and spoons. The whole thing looked so costly and so orderly that Lucy wondered how Mother could bear to put in the usual jar of lemon juice and sugar for the lemonade, the pan of fried chicken, the covered bowl of potato salad, and over everything the mended blue-and-white tablecloth.

"No room in the auto for an Owen today, because we'll bring back new china," Mother said. "Anyway, Gwin's coming over to take Topsy for a run, isn't she?"

"Yes, and she's promised not to let her out of the yard," Lucy answered. "I'm so afraid, Mother, about Topsy getting distemper."

"That's one thing you're right to fear, Lucy," said Father, coming into the kitchen. "Carl Torsen says Rip has it now." Father carried the lunch case out to the Regal, with Lucy beside him, holding the boxed cake. "It's good you kept Rip out of our yard. It was worth a chop."

Lucy and Mother sat in the back seat so that Mother could guard the cake. There was a strong prairie wind, but Father had folded down the black cloth top of the auto—"Fresh air never hurt anybody," he said. Lucy noticed that Mother had four long hatpins crisscrossed to hold on her hat.

After Amory opened and closed the driveway gate and climbed into the front seat, they were off. They jounced and bumped along several miles on the road toward Hannah and the Canadian border, until they came to a one-room country school with fifteen or twenty children playing outdoors for recess. Father slowed, and they all waved to the children and the young girl-teacher in the doorway.

"That's Mary Hoffer and the school where she's teaching this summer," he told Mother. "I think she's a crackerjack of a teacher, but old man Hoffer won't send her to normal school to get a diploma."

"And she's had such a hard life," Mother said. "She was only nine years old when her mother died with that last baby. She's slaved for those brothers ever since. Can't you lend her a little so she can go away, Harry?" Mother asked.

Then while Mother and Father discussed money, Lucy thought of the death of Mary's mother. It made her cold all over just to think of it. What would she do if her own mother died? Would she manage as well as Mary had? Never! She knew she couldn't.

On the last acres in the States, right on the Canadian border, Father stopped to talk to a farmer, who left his team and binder and came over to the road. Lucy got out with her camera and walked the few yards to the cement post that marked the line between the two countries.

As she focused for her snapshot, she realized that a cement post only three or four feet high with open prairie all around it wouldn't make a very exciting picture. But she snapped it, and climbing back into the auto, she said to Mother, "I'm counting on getting a picture of my Mounty, Sergeant McHenry, today. He looks so grand on his horse."

"How would you like me to take a picture of you with him?" Mother asked. "I don't think he'd object."

"I'll bet the horse will be better-looking than old roaring boring Lucy." Amory had to say something. He'd been quiet most of the way.

Father came back. "Paul Totten says that Canada is getting much stricter about crossing the border, because of the war," he said. "So we'll stop at Snowflake and report."

"Oh, yes, Harry, don't take any chances. All these years we've just crossed wherever and whenever we liked, but now we must obey the law. They're at war." Mother spoke very seriously.

"Sooner or later we'll be in it, too." Father lifted his hand for a moment from the wheel and motioned toward the fields. "Look—this wonderful harvest, and the boys going off to war before the crop is in."

"And some will never come back," Mother added mournfully. "Mr. Owen says that men are sent to the front before they've even finished training—to die in the trenches."

"But the Allies will win!" Amory exclaimed.

"What's the good of winning if you're dead?" Lucy asked. In her imagination she saw long lines of men on muddy country roads, all marching toward big guns that blew them to bits.

By now they were in Snowflake, Manitoba, a little cluster of houses around one tall grain elevator. They stopped at a low wooden building with the British flag and the Canadian flag both flying from the white pole in front of it.

Amory didn't bother to get out. Instead he opened

his *Boys' Life* and started to read an adventure story. Mother stayed where she was, holding the cake. But Lucy jumped out to follow Father.

Ever since the time three or four years before when the red-haired Sergeant McHenry, wearing a scarlet jacket and riding a beautiful horse, had helped Father mend a flat tire, Lucy had thought of him as her own Mounty. Whenever he met them on Sundays on their way to picnics, he always joked, saying, "My red-haired girl again! Why don't you grow up faster so we can get married?"

He was always riding on the roads, so in the tiny office Lucy wasn't surprised to see a middle-aged man with bushy white eyebrows. He sat stiffly behind the desk, listening closely while Father explained that they were going to Crystal City to buy china and then to the Pembina River for a picnic.

Since Lucy was now at the desk also, Father laughed and said, "Here's my daughter, looking for her own special Mounty. Better watch out, or she'll follow the Mounty motto and get her man. It's your red-haired Sergeant McHenry she's after. Seen him lately?"

The man's lined face tightened, as he looked sharply at Father and then at Lucy. "You'll not see our Sergeant McHenry ever again," he said hoarsely. "He's dead. Killed in the big push on the Somme. He was—" And the man could not go on. He bent his head and pulled out the wide drawer in front of him, pretending to ruffle through some papers.

At first, Father seemed not to know what to say. Then he spoke very solemnly. "He was a good man. He helped us once, and he never forgot us, so well— we'll never forget him either."

He took Lucy by the hand and led her out to the

auto. She had begun to cry very softly to herself.

Mother saw them come out and noticed how for-lorn Lucy was. "Won't they let us go to Crystal City? And Lucy, don't look so woebegone. If we can't go today, there are always other days."

"But there aren't any other days for Sergeant Mc-Henry," Lucy said and began to sob.

"Where is he, Harry?" Mother asked quietly. She helped Lucy in, handed her a clean handkerchief, and then put her arm around her.

"Killed in the Battle of the Somme," Father an-swered grimly.

"The biggest battle ever, wasn't it?" Amory asked him.

"Yes, the most men slaughtered, though the armies are enormous. So maybe the record for the proportion of men dying is still with Gettysburg, where my father fought."

Lucy pushed closer to Mother, covered her face with the handkerchief, and wished they'd stop talking about records for slaughter. Sometimes only Mother was a comfort.

After that, the day wasn't the same, though the Regal bounced along as jouncily as ever, the sun still lit the yellow fields of grain, and Crystal City, when they came to it, was almost as good as its name sug-gested. There were brick stores, brick houses with lawns, and even a few iron fences around the yards. The streets weren't rutted, the trees on either side were planted in shady rows, and the sidewalks were made of concrete instead of boards.

In the china shop, Mother found her own china pattern and began to select cups and saucers. Yet to Lucy everything was a little sad.

"You should have been here to celebrate Dominion Day," the salesman said. "Three bands and three companies of soldiers marching, men from around here—Pilot Mound and Purves and Snowflake and all the farms. Gone now, shipped across the country and off to war. The armies are dreadful short of men, we hear —so many dead already."

Mother went on choosing perfect cups and saucers; Father asked about the crops; and Amory asked about the fishing; but Lucy thought of Luke Morgan, the one Canadian soldier she knew. And the fear of war grew bigger and bigger in her mind.

Father noticed her doleful expression and suggested, "How about buying Lucy that little pitcher for her stone house?"

"Hey, it's a picnic for my birthday, not hers!"

"Want some china, Amory?" Father grinned. "How about a tea set for your Cave Men?"

"Not that junk! But I saw a store across the street that sells fishing stuff."

"All right. You pick your pitcher, Lucy. Here's the money you'll need, Caroline. I'll go buy hooks with Amory." And Father was gone. Obviously Father also preferred fishing tackle to dishes.

The little white pitcher with a brown lamb painted on it made Lucy forget the war and the dying. She already saw the pitcher on her small clubhouse table, and the Stone Age Girls having a party.

Later, they arrived at their picnic spot on the Pembina, a favorite of Lucy's. Always shady and with a view of the river, it had low hills on three sides so that you felt protected. The campfire was always in the same circle of stones, with the same notched sticks ready for the hanging kettle. Everything was as it always was, and Lucy loved it.

Yet she kept hearing, "You'll not see our Sergeant McHenry ever again." She forgot it while she ate potato salad and drank her cup of lemonade. Then she heard it again; it went in and out of her mind all the rest of the day.

When it was time to cut the cake, Amory let out a howl. "No candles? I'll have bad luck the whole year!"

"You're the luckiest one in the family. You win every game I play with you. You win when you take chances on anything. You always get what you want for Christmas, and—and I just wish I could have your luck! And yesterday when I blew out my birthday candles, that Edward blew first, and now I don't even get that luck." The more Lucy talked, the sadder she felt, for herself, for her Mounty, and for everything. She was almost crying.

"For goodness' sakes," Mother scolded. "You're not that unlucky, Lucy. And Amory, you have your cake. Now eat it!"

At that, they all laughed, for Father always said about Amory, "He's the boy who can eat his cake and have it, too."

Later, while Father caught one fish and Amory caught a whole string of them, Mother and Lucy walked through the woods to the nearby farm where they always went for more drinking water. At first no one seemed to be at home, but as they began to pump, a pale young woman with pale-blue eyes and pale-tan freckles came to the back door.

Mother stopped pumping. "We thought everybody was away," she explained.

"They are all away," the woman said, only she

didn't say *away*. She said *awiy*, so it rhymed with *high*. "I shut up tight," she went on. "I'm alwiys afride. These woods, no people, no streets, no 'ouses."

"You're new here, aren't you?" Mother asked gently.

"I'm stright from London. Wish I was back there. I married my soldier, and he died in the trenches. Then 'is folks said, 'Come live 'ere, in Canada.' But I'm afride. I 'ate it 'ere."

And to Lucy she looked frightened, her eyes never at rest but glancing constantly at the trees and under-brush and the open barnyard. She stood warily, half in and half out of the door, and she soon backed into the house. Before she shut herself in, she put her mouth to the crack of doorway remaining open and almost whispered, "These woods and the dark nights —I wish I was 'ome." Lucy barely heard the last two faint words. "I'm afride." And the door closed.

On the way back to the picnic spot, Lucy asked Mother, "There's more wrong with her than just being afraid, isn't there?"

"We can't judge," Mother answered. "Perhaps back in London she'd be all right. Here everything is strange to her, even her husband's folks. Women can be war casualties, too, you know."

When the fishing was done and the early supper was eaten, they packed up. Then, loaded with their empty picnic suitcase, the blanket, the kettle, and Amory's string of fish, they went through the woods to the auto.

This end of a picnic day was Lucy's favorite time to ride. As they came closer and closer to Wales, Lucy felt more and more secure. It was dusk when Wales finally came into sight.

From that side of the village, she saw the six grain elevators first, but once they had turned onto the road past her house, Lucy saw their five cottonwoods, the branches moving slightly in the evening breeze. Amory jumped out, dangling his half-wrapped string of fish, and opened the driveway gate. Father drove in beside the house, clicked off the engine, and Lucy could hear, ever so clearly, the rustle of the stiff cottonwood leaves.

"Crystal City was nice," she said to Mother as they sat for a moment. "But for all the brick houses and lawns, I wouldn't want to live there and be at war, would you?"

"You are lucky, then, aren't you?" Mother answered.

"No northern lights tonight, so let's go in," Father said. "You must be very tired, Caroline."

"Not too tired—just glad to be home."

And Lucy felt the same way, exactly.

Water Pistols

~~~

"One, two, three." On the front porch, having finished her Saturday morning chores, Lucy was counting for Topsy to waltz in her new black satin bonnet and cape. "You do look smart in that costume," Lucy praised her, but Topsy ignored the compliment. She had her eye on the bit of cake that Lucy held for reward.

Mother came in from the flower garden, carrying a bunch of pink and red sweet William. "More flowers to deliver, Lucy. To Mrs. Bortz this time," Mother said. "I'm going to lie down until it's time to cook dinner."

"Are you sick or something? You never used to lie down all the time. And you don't get any better either." Lucy tried not to sound too worried.

"I'll be better later on, dear. Don't you worry about me." And Mother went into the living room, while Lucy took off Topsy's outfit, picked up the bunch of flowers, and went around the house to the back walk.

Almost at the gate, she noticed that Topsy was following her. "No, Topsy, you stay home," Lucy ordered. And because she always talked to Topsy as a person, she explained. "Distemper germs are everywhere now. Yesterday Rip Torsen died of it." She took Topsy back and shut her in the shed.

Mrs. Bortz had been very ill ever since she had heard that both her German nephews had been killed. Lucy was about to knock softly on the front door, when Dr. Stewart of Langdon stepped out. He was talking to the young woman who came with him to the door.

"I find her much better today, so I'll not come again. Anyway, Dr. Carmer should soon be back in Wales."

Lucy quickly handed the flowers to the young woman. "Tell Mrs. Bortz that the flowers are from my mother, Mrs. Johnston."

"Oh, so you're the Johnstons' little girl?" Dr. Stewart asked. "I saw you when you were born, and a relative of ours came to nurse you and your mother. Did you know about that?"

Ordinarily Lucy would have said only a "Yes," but this time she felt lucky to meet him. "My mother was going to write you, Dr. Stewart, for Miss Ross's address. We want to ask her what the spell is on me, or whether it's done now. I'm eleven, you know, and the northern lights change every eleven years."

Dr. Stewart stared at her as though she were a complete muddlehead. "Just a minute. What in the mischief is this about northern lights and a spell? Is your mother into witchcraft?" He peered at Lucy through his steel-rimmed glasses.

"Your relative, Miss Ross, said I was born under the spell of the northern lights because they were so bright the night I was born, but nobody asked her what she meant. And I'd like to know—wouldn't you if you were me?"

"Well, if Janet Ross said it, she must have meant something. She has a lot of strange ideas. Why don't you write her?" He started for his auto. "Come along. I'll write her address for you."

In the front seat of his Ford, he pulled his prescription pad from his bag, and saying the address aloud to Lucy, word by word, he wrote: "Miss Janet Ross, 110 High Street, Fort Augustus, Inverness, Scotland."

When he handed it to Lucy, she asked, "Will it take long to hear from her? I really do want to know."

"Haven't felt yourself shrinking lately, have you?" He spoke in his doctor's voice, but at the same time he grinned. "A shrinking spell would be a total disaster for you. Then there's the spell of sleeping a hundred years—been very sleepy lately? Or how about Beauty and the Beast—aren't in love with any monster are you?"

Lucy caught on to his jokes. "I'm growing a little instead of shrinking, but I do love a beast. It's my dog Topsy, only I don't think she rates as a monster. She's only so big," and Lucy put her hands about twelve inches apart.

"Looks like a rare case that I can't diagnose," he said in a serious tone. "You'll have to write Janet Ross, though don't expect a quick reply. German submarines are sinking ships at a great rate."

He snapped shut his bag, went around to the front of his auto, cranked it violently, got in, and yelled at Lucy, "Get out of the way! This rampaging beast could run you down!"

Lucy ran across the road, waved good-bye, and raced home. "Mother, I've got Miss Ross's address from Dr. Stewart. Won't you get up and write her?"

Mother opened the flap of her spindly-legged desk, and as usual old letters and address books and cards tumbled out on the floor. While Lucy picked them up, Mother sat down and talked as she wrote:

"Dear Miss Ross,
We often think of you, and our Lucy has a request to make. She wants to know—"

Mother handed Lucy another sheet of paper. "You write your own note, dear. It will sound better from you."

Since Lucy had only the spell-question to ask, her note was very brief, so she added a *P.S. I've got hair now and it's red.* Miss Ross must have a very unfavorable memory of her looks—"A big mouth and not a spear of hair," Mother had said.

"Why not take this to the post office right now," Mother said as she addressed the envelope and sealed it. "And I want you to take this note to Nora Butler. They've no phone. I hear she's coming home from that farm where she's been working. I'd like her to help when I have the Ladies Aid. She's a hard worker; the only Butler worth her salt."

Lucy set off, first to the post office and then to the Butlers' run-down place on the far side of town. The Butlers' yard was always full of molting chickens, dirty little boys, and a mangy dog or two. At the sagging gate, Mrs. Butler, herself rather sagging, met Lucy. "Back from your trip? How's your ma? You stay puny, don't you? Same age as my Gracie, but she's a lot fatter than you."

Then she looked at the note Lucy gave her, and saw it was for Nora, her oldest girl. "Tell your ma Nora ain't home yet. Sent word she's coming, though. All of us is moving to Canada, the Northwest. Going on the train, soon's we get money."

Mrs. Butler was good for an hour of talk if you let her go on, so Lucy interrupted. "I'll tell my mother about Nora." And she ran down the dirt road to Main Street.

As Lucy approached her own back door, Amory emerged from his cave, ran to the tub of water at the pump, and as he filled his water pistol, he yelled, "Stick 'em up or I'll shoot!" He was only a few feet from her and couldn't possibly miss.

For once, instead of running into the house, Lucy dashed at Amory, snatched the water pistol from him, and yelled as loud as he had. "You stick 'em up! I'll souse you! I will!"

The whole proceeding was so unexpected that Amory did put up his hands, howling, "Don't shoot! It's a clean shirt!" Then Lucy looked so determined and the full water pistol was so close to his face that he ducked and circled around her to the garden. In the one second that he ducked, Lucy made her great mistake.

She pulled the trigger. The water squirted in one great spray and hit Father full in the face. He had been coming from the garden, and she hadn't noticed him.

"Luuuucy!" he bellowed. "What are you doing?"

He grew redder and redder in the face. "You've soaked my collar and my jacket and my shirt! And whose gun is that?"

"It's Amory's," Lucy said in a panic. "And I didn't mean to hit you. I just got tired of Amory always doing things to me."

Amory now came out of the currant bushes where he'd been hiding. "I wouldn't have shot you, Lucy. I was only going to scare you into the house."

"I'm not going to be scared of you anymore, so now!" She tossed him the pistol. "Next time I get it, I'll shoot you instead of Father," she threatened.

"I should hope so," Father said angrily. "Amory, don't let me see that gun in this yard again. You give it away, and no arguments." Then his mood changed, and he began to laugh.

"What a girl! I encourage you to have spunk and you shoot me with a water pistol." But the mention of water made him cross again. He went into the house, pulling off his wet jacket. Both Amory and Lucy waited a few minutes, and then they slipped quietly into the kitchen while Father was upstairs changing. Mother was dishing up dinner, and she was smiling to herself.

"Not afraid of anything, are you, Lucy?" she teased.

That noon Father was not in a very good mood, so at first everyone ate without much table talk. But finally, Amory must have thought Father was soothed. "Stan's going out to work on a farm," Amory began. "I want to go earn cash, too. Will you let me go?" He sat watching Father's face very closely.

"What do you think, Caroline?" Father was undecided.

"It depends on the farm. If he could go out to Nick Schneider's, that's not far and they have boys of their own," Mother spoke slowly.

"Good idea! That's a place where they'd keep an eye on him." Father paused, and then he both scolded and joked, "The trouble is that it takes more than an eye to watch Amory."

"And after I'm in practice, I might earn a dollar a day, and if I work until school begins, I'll have twenty, twenty-five, thirty—"

"Hold on! You haven't earned a cent yet!" Father reminded him. "First thing we know, you'll have spent twenty dollars before you've earned twenty cents."

"Am I glad to miss that Ladies Aid stampede," Amory said, shrilly. "Get me out of here before that mob scene," he begged.

"Not a very nice way to refer to your mother's church gathering," Father said. But he did arrange for Amory to work on the Schneiders' farm, staying there nights, also.

The Stone Age Girls spent the three days before the Ladies Aid working for Mother. They rubbed the silver spoons and forks; they waxed the floors; they washed the teacups, new and old, including the set that came from Japan and had a different bird painted on every piece. And Lucy climbed on a high stool to hand down from a top shelf the special party plates—pale green with carved rabbits on them.

While she was poking about on that high shelf, Lucy moved things around, searching for that hard-to-hide secret the folks had talked about. But whatever it was, it wasn't hidden there. So the secret remained a secret.

On the afternoon of the Aid meeting, Joey Dahl's mother came nearly half an hour early. Since Mother was changing her clothes, Lucy welcomed her in. "Can I take your hat upstairs?" Lucy offered.

"No, I'm keeping it on," Mrs. Dahl said softly. "Has your mama got a Sears catalog?"

"Of course," Lucy replied, and quickly brought the catalog.

Mrs. Dahl flipped the pages, came to women's hats, and Lucy, looking at the pictures, saw that Mrs. Dahl was checking her own hat, a flat black straw with a huge red satin bow across the front.

"We don't have a catalog of our own, but I was sure I was right." Mrs. Dahl patted her hat more firmly on her head. "You just see when Mrs. Towne comes. She's wearing the exact same hat, back side around. Imagine that, doesn't know how to wear a hat!" Mrs. Dahl sniffed. "It spoils my pleasure in wearing my own, but I won't tell her, I won't. I'll just keep mine on." Mrs. Dahl went into the living room and plumped herself down in the most comfortable chair.

In a few moments, Lucy called to Mother, who was now in the kitchen, "Here they come, ahead of time! Get your apron off!" Lucy swung open the screen door to let them all in. Mr. Quimby had brought Mrs. Quimby, and the back seat was jammed with three wide women. Mr. Flint had taken time off to drive Mrs. Flint and Morrie and Dorrie around the block to the Johnstons'.

Mr. and Mrs. Owen came along the back walk with their four children, but they circled the house to come in the front door, since this was a church occasion. And Mrs. Smith got out of their black buggy

at the gate, saying something to Roger before he snapped the reins and drove off. Roger was only fourteen, but Lucy admired everything about him, from his blond, curly hair to his grown-up ways.

Everybody carried a box or a tray or a plate; and the round cakes, the square cakes, the jelly rolls, and the decorated cupcakes made the children want to eat at once.

Hearing an auto honk, Lucy ran out to open the big gate. It was Mrs. Kane and her three little boys in their new Ford, which Mrs. Kane was learning to drive. The gate was barely open when the Ford came careening through.

"I can't stop it! I can't stop it!" shrieked Mrs. Kane, as the autoful of Kanes whizzed past Lucy and raced toward the stone house. Lucy held her breath,

and Mother, who had come out to welcome Mrs. Kane, put her hands over her eyes.

Then eight-year-old Johnnie, who was known as a "holy terror," but who did understand the Ford, jerked up the emergency brake, and they halted, six inches from the wall of the stone house.

The last to arrive was Mrs. Towne. She stopped her horse and buggy in front of the house and called, "Taking the horse to the livery stable. Leave some cake for me." And she set off briskly toward Main Street. Soon she had walked back from town, came breezily in the back door, put the biggest cake of all on the dining-room table, and went to sit in the living room, with a loud "Hello, everybody."

It was true! She wore her hat back side around. Lucy noted how superior Mrs. Dahl looked, but she could also see that Mrs. Towne never glanced at the other hat, and she wouldn't have cared if she had. She was a widow who ran her own farm and made money on it, Father said. Lucy liked her because she always treated her like another woman and not a child.

For the next hour the girls tried to keep track of the small children out in the yard, while indoors the ladies had a prayer meeting. The few little girls were happy in the stone house, but the three Kane boys and Morrie and Edward gathered around the cover on Amory's cave.

"What's under that?" asked Johnnie Kane.

"It's a deep dark cave, and I fell into it once," said Morrie.

"So did I," said Edward, not to be outdone. "You boys want a turn to fall in?" Lucy overheard him and came running. The five boys were already wrestling with the heavy wooden cover.

"Nobody is having a turn falling in today—nobody!" she shouted. "You can do absolutely anything you like, but stay away from Amory's cave," she ordered. They went off toward the tall weeds beside the barn.

Before long, Mother called everyone in, the children to have cake and the Stone Age Girls to pass the cakes, the cups of coffee, the lumps of sugar, and the pitchers of yellow cream. For a moment, Lucy wondered why Nora Butler wasn't there to do it. Mother had asked her in the note. But maybe she wasn't home yet. She'd have to ask, but not now. Mother gave the boys each a great wedge of chocolate cake and sent them out to play again. And the girls stayed inside.

Everything went smoothly in the living room—a

soft murmur of women talking and of spoons and forks on saucers and plates.

Then Dorrie Flint noticed some of the women had plates with bunnies on them and hers was a bird plate. "Lucy, gimme a bunny. You gave a bunny plate to Mrs. Towne and not to me!"

Dorrie began to throw one of her yelling fits. Mrs. Flint only smiled, so Lucy explained, "We have only six with bunnies, Dorrie, and people are eating off them." She wanted to turn Dorrie upside down and spank her, but it seemed unwise.

"I want a bunny!" Dorrie howled again, and the next instant she grabbed for Mrs. Towne's plate.

Mrs. Towne firmly clutched her plate, glared at Dorrie, and spoke. "Little girl, it's time you learned some manners. You eat from your bird plate and let's not have another yap out of you." Mrs. Towne stopped talking and went on eating cake from her green bunny plate. And the wonder was that Dorrie also stopped, began to eat, and stared at Mrs. Towne with round eyes.

It was Mrs. Flint who was shocked, and Lucy thought there might be a fracas right in the living room. But nothing happened, only a long silence, with everyone quietly concentrating on eating cake. Then Mr. Owen cleared his throat and announced, "We should have one more hymn before we go. Any suggestions?"

"Let's have a good loud rousing one," said Mrs. Towne, who was never bashful. "I need that kind before I go home to feed the pigs and milk the cows."

Mr. Owen looked as though he'd never heard of such animals, let alone having to feed them. But

Mother went to the piano and said, "Why don't we stand up and sing 'Onward, Christian Soldiers.' That's a loud and rousing one."

They had sung only those first words, when war whoops and battle cries came from the backyard. Mrs. Flint stopped singing and spoke out, right above the music. "Is my Morrie out there? Where's my Morrie?" She had her answer in no time.

In the back door dashed Morrie and Edward, both screaming, and after them came the three Kanes, yelling, "We gotcha! We gotcha!"

They raced through the kitchen, into the living room, over the ladies' feet, around the two rocking chairs, and out the front door. Each of the three Kanes held an enormous water pistol, much larger than any Amory had ever had. The Kanes were only slightly damp, but Morrie and Edward were dripping wet.

The ladies sang on, but Mrs. Flint took off after the line of boys. "Morrie! Morrie!" she shrieked.

Then Gwen, Gwin, and Guinevere tore out the door after Mrs. Flint, all moaning, "Edward, Edward!" Lucy was about to follow, when she suddenly had a better idea. She ran to the back screen door, stood outside it, and waited for the battle line to approach again. In an instant, it came, head on into Lucy.

"Stop!" she screamed. But they couldn't stop, at least not until they had piled up against her and she had fallen through the screen, smashing it out of its frame. She kicked and shoved the five boys off her, picked herself up, and wondered what Father would say about the screen. But everyone was worried about the boys and not the broken door.

The Owen girls were cuddling Edward, who was

sobbing, "They didn't tell us they had three water pistols!"

"It wasn't fair," Morrie wept. "Amory gave me just one."

"Poor, poor little Morrie," Mrs. Flint comforted him.

"They shot us first," complained Johnnie. "We're never coming here again." And he took his brothers off to the Ford, to wait there until the meeting was over.

Lucy's dress was ripped on one shoulder, but she was too tired to care. Back in the living room, Mr. Owen was saying a final prayer. But only Mr. and Mrs. Owen had their eyes closed. Every other woman was looking around with half-closed eyes, wondering what might happen next.

That night at supper, Father first asked Mother how she felt, then he grumbled about the broken screen door. Finally he stared at Lucy, who was sitting with her eyes down, trying to be invisible.

"By jiminy jinks!" he burst out. "Instead of my raising a rumpus, I should compliment you on your spunk. You saved the Ladies Aid from a shoot-out."

The Butler Baby

~~~⌘~~~

One afternoon not long after that, Lucy hurried out to clean the stone house for a meeting of the Stone Age Girls. She had barely put the two small rockers and the red scatter rugs out in the sun, when Mother called, "Lucy, please come and do an errand for me."

Lucy went back inside the stone house just long enough to say, as loud as she dared, "Rats! Darned blasted RATS!" After that she went indoors. "Amory's home from the farm today. Why can't he ever do an errand?"

"He's off with the boys—they're all in town to-day," Mother answered. "Anyway, Amory's no use for an emergency errand. He finds so many things to do along the way that the emergency is over before he gets there." Mother was ramming all kinds of clean old cloths into a big flour sack as she talked.

"What's the emergency?" Lucy asked.

Mother didn't reply, only stood thinking. "I get so dizzy nowadays when I climb up that ladder to the barn loft that you'll have to go for me, Lucy."

"You call that an emergency?" Lucy asked again.

"No. But you climb up, open that first gray trunk you come to, and on top you'll find a sealed paper package labeled DIAPERS. Don't pinch your fingers when that heavy trunk cover slams down, and don't fall off the ladder, and don't dawdle."

Mother noticed Lucy's puzzled expression and laughed. "That is a lot of *don'ts* for one trip, but do be careful."

"I don't mind the *don'ts*. But what's the emergency? And whose diapers are they?"

"They're nobody's diapers now. You know, Lucy, my last three babies were born too soon and didn't live. But this afternoon a new baby is coming at the Butlers', and Mrs. Sanderson is going over to help. She wants clean cloths. Mrs. Butler never has anything ready."

"I suppose it will be another boy," Lucy said with disgust. "Mrs. Butler's last five have been boys. But Nora and Gracie and Aggie—I bet they want a baby girl for a little sister. And I wonder what they'll name her."

"How you do run on, my dear. Go along and get the diapers, and I'll look for another sheet we can spare." And Mother went upstairs.

The barn ladder was only a few boards, spaced rather far apart and nailed to the wall two-by-fours. The opening above had a trap door, which everyone was warned to close, but no one bothered.

Lucy climbed up, finding as usual that her legs were barely long enough to stretch from one board to the next. In the hot loft, streaks of dusty sunbeams came through the cracks and around the big window at one end. Since the Johnstons had no horses or cows, the loft was their storage attic and had not held hay for years. Yet it had a dry hayseed smell that mixed with the odor of mothballs when Lucy pushed up the heavy trunk top.

There was the package, just as Mother had said, but Lucy couldn't resist running her hand along a narrow, tightly wrapped package under it. Whatever it was, she'd never seen it before. "This might be the secret that's so hard to hide," she said to herself, as she tore away a piece of the brown paper.

But it couldn't possibly be for her. It was a rifle, so it must be for Amory for Christmas. If the folks were giving him something so expensive, her own secret present must be very special, she decided, as she slammed down the cover of the trunk.

She hated going down that loft ladder backward, especially when she had only one hand free, but step by step she slowly climbed down, and once she was on the barn floor again, she ran to the house.

Mother held the flour sack open, Lucy pushed the diaper package in, and Mother tied a string around the top. "Think you can manage it, Lucy?" she asked. "It's bigger and heavier than I expected. I'd go, but I feel sick to my stomach today."

With the big flour sack Lucy couldn't run, but she did hurry the three blocks to the Sandersons' neat little house. When she knocked, no one was home, but Mrs. Torsen came out of her house next door. "Mr. Butler came over and said the baby was coming so fast that Mrs. Sanderson's already gone," she explained.

Since she liked the idea of going closer to the excitement, even if it was at the Butlers' house, Lucy went on, though the sack was getting heavy in her arms. She pushed open the Butlers' gate, and at the back door she had to push aside two-year-old Buddy and three-year-old Joey, who were leaning against the torn screen, both of them sucking their thumbs.

Lucy then rapped loudly on the door, expecting Mrs. Sanderson to come. But when the door opened, Lucy was so astonished that at first she couldn't say a word.

It was Mrs. Butler who stood in front of her—fully dressed, not sick, and certainly not having a baby. Lucy's mouth opened, but she said nothing, only put the flour sack in Mrs. Butler's arms.

Then Mrs. Butler opened her mouth, and plenty of words came out. "Things from your ma? That's good! She's always got something, and always good things, too. Now what did she put in this bag?" And she began to untie the top.

But before she had time to go on, Mrs. Sanderson, in her white nursing outfit, came to the door. When she looked over Mrs. Butler's shoulder and saw Lucy, she said, "Thank you, Lucy. Now run along home. Tell your mother I'll phone her when I'm done here." She reached around Mrs. Butler and shut the door.

Lucy had never been more puzzled. She rushed home and burst into the living room, where Mother lay on the sofa. "Mother, there's been a mistake," Lucy began, breathlessly. "When I got to Sandersons', Mr. Butler had already called for Mrs. Sanderson because the baby was coming so fast. So I went to Butlers', and Mrs. Butler—Mother, would you answer the door if you were going to have a baby any minute?"

Mother slowly sat up and said, "Come sit here on the rocker beside me." When Lucy was sitting next to her, Mother went on. "You're right. Mrs. Butler is not having a baby today, but there is a Butler baby being born."

"Whose baby is it, then?" Lucy asked.

"It's Nora's. You know that babies are sometimes born to girls who aren't married. Nora came home from the country last night, and today she's having a baby at her house."

"Nora having a baby? She's old, but she's not that old, is she? Why, she's only sixteen. Are you sure she's having a baby?" Lucy was thunderstruck. "And who's that baby's father? And where is he?"

"Mrs. Sanderson thinks the baby's father has skipped," Mother said.

"Skipped?" asked Lucy. "Skipped what?"

"Skipped out of the county, probably. He was the hired man at that farm where she worked. Poor Nora —she's never had a chance. Mrs. Sanderson says that Nora didn't really understand. She thought the hired man would marry her. There was nobody to tell her anything, and the hired man may have been nice to her."

"Nice to her!" exclaimed Lucy. "He skips and leaves her with a baby!" Then she thought a moment. "What will Nora do with a baby?"

"That's one thing you needn't worry about," Mother answered. "In a village like this, the girl's mother brings up the baby with her own children.

After a while everyone will just think of it as the youngest Butler." Lucy's face must have shown what she thought of Mrs. Butler's way of bringing up children, for Mother went on.

"Of course it's not ideal, but it means that Nora can watch her baby grow up. Now one thing more. There'll be a lot of gossip about all this, and even the Owen girls will hear of it. All you need to say is that we don't think it was poor Nora's fault. And if you have any more questions, ask me—not anyone else."

Lucy still had questions—dozens of them—but Mother lay down again, closed her eyes, and that finished the conversation.

Out at the stone house, Lucy swept and cleaned, but it didn't seem as exciting as it had. She was imagining what it would be like to have a baby of her own. Eventually she lifted her treasure box from the sill where she kept it, inserted the key in the tiny padlock, and clicked the top open. One by one, she lifted out her treasures. There was a sliver of birch bark and a beautiful pink stone from the Pembina, a piece of Ivory soap wrapped in paper with HOTEL FARGO printed on it, a silver button with PARIS inscribed around the back, and the spoon with their Majesties on the handle.

Underneath was a layer of cotton. And under that she had put her five-dollar gold piece. She lifted the cotton now to gloat on the golden coin. But the gold piece was not there.

She shook the cotton; she unrolled the bit of birch bark; she turned the box upside down; she searched the sill and then the floor. She even unwrapped the little bar of soap. There was no five-dollar gold piece anywhere. A thief must have opened her box and stolen her treasure. A burglar!

The entire meeting of the Stone Age club that afternoon was spent discussing who might have taken it and when and how.

"Could be the Cave Men," suggested Gwen, "but Amory's been away, hasn't he?"

"More likely those awful Kane boys that were so rude to our Edward," said Guinevere.

"No, I'll bet it was an out-and-out burglar," Gwin said. "A town like this must have a gang of thieves that stole your thimble, too."

"I don't know," Lucy said uncertainly, hating to think there might be real burglars in Wales. "Funny things do go on in this town," and as she said it, she thought of Nora Butler. But since they didn't know the baby was being born, Lucy didn't explain what she meant.

At suppertime, Lucy took the treasure box up to her room, but she didn't bother to lock it. Now she had only one of her golden presents left, her gold locket. She put that under her pile of long stockings in the bottom drawer, and went down to set the table. Sooner or later she'd have to confess she'd lost both the gold thimble and the five-dollar gold piece.

Amory was home for supper and was going back that night to the farm. "Boys like me are doing men's work," he bragged. Then he added, "But so far I'm getting only seventy-five cents a day, and the first days only fifty."

"I told Nick to pay you what you were worth, Amory, and you're not a man yet. But he says you have buckled down very well." Father for once sounded proud of Amory.

On the strength of Father's praise, Amory took

three of the biggest ears of corn and most of the butter on the butter plate. Then as he buttered and salted his corn, he began to talk.

"Did you hear that Nora Butler had a baby girl a couple of hours ago? And she's not even married. And Jerry and I wondered if there'd be a shotgun wedding and—"

"Yes, Amory, we know about it," Mother interrupted him.

"And Stan says there's not a chance, because the hired man at the farm has skipped the county—so, well, I suppose there won't be a shotgun wedding after all." Amory sounded very disappointed.

But Lucy was only puzzled. "A shotgun wedding? What's that?"

"That's my roaring boring sister! Doesn't even know about weddings," he jeered at her.

"I do know a lot about weddings, wedding dresses, bridesmaids, wedding cakes, and—" Lucy paused, realizing that none of these things included a shotgun. She turned to Father. "What's it mean?" she asked.

"Well, your mother has explained some things to you today, I hear, so I'll explain this one," Father began, reaching for a fresh cinnamon roll before Amory had time to take his fourth.

"Long ago, Lucy, if a baby was born to a girl who didn't have a husband and her father knew who the father of the baby was, he'd go and threaten the man with a shotgun until he promised to marry the girl. Then she'd have a husband, and the baby would have a father."

"What a terrible way to get married!" Lucy gasped.

"Nowadays people don't use shotguns for anything but hunting, dear," Mother said.

"Yeah, and we boys think Mr. Butler doesn't even have a shotgun, and anyway he's such a feeble old carcass that—"

"We'll change the subject, Amory," Father stated so definitely that Amory shut up. "What went on at your meeting of the club today, Lucy?" Father asked.

"An awful thing has happened," she began. Then thinking of Nora and her baby, Lucy changed her opening. "Well, it's awful to me, anyway. Somebody stole my five-dollar gold piece." As she said it, she took a quick look at Father and then at Mother to gauge their shock or disapproval. They'd probably call her careless, and Mother did begin that way.

"You must have mislaid it," she said. "Absolutely no one around here is a thief."

"Was it lying around, Lucy, so that anyone could pick it up?" Father asked. Then he added, "Just to admire it, perhaps?" so he wouldn't contradict Mother.

"It was locked in my birthday treasure box that Mr. Owen made, and I kept it hidden," Lucy went on. "But the last time I saw it was a couple of days before the Ladies Aid came and—"

"Whoa, Lucy," Father teased. "You're not going to blame the Methodist Ladies Aid for a break-in, are you? Caroline, did you notice any suspicious actions —any ladies slipping out to the stone house during prayers and hymns, for instance?"

Amory was now intently buttering his fifth ear of corn and saying nothing.

"You know I don't mean any of the women," Lucy said disgustedly. "But there were all those children, and those Kane boys are terrors—you say that yourself, Mother."

"But if your box was locked and the key was hidden, no boy could possibly steal from it," Mother reminded Lucy.

"That Johnnie Kane did it, I'm sure—he's the worst," Lucy argued. "Could I go to their house and just ask him? He took it—I'm sure."

"No, he didn't," Amory said. "I did."

"You stole it? Amory Johnston, what kind of shenanigans is that!" Father scowled and glared and roared at the same time. "I've put up with a lot, but I will not put up with stealing!"

"How could you, Amory?" Mother asked sadly.

"Why did you take it? And give it back to me, right now!" Lucy shouted at him.

"I wanted to show that your measly little lock on that box wasn't foolproof, so I opened it with a wire, after I saw the box in your stone house."

"You pick locks as well as steal?" Father boomed, growing more and more red in the face.

"Anyway, you just hand it over," Lucy demanded, holding out her hand.

"I haven't got it now," Amory said faintly. "I lost it."

"You lost my gold coin? Where?" shrieked Lucy.

"Well, it's a long story—"

"You make it a quick one," Father barked.

"And I'm earning the money to pay you back." Amory smiled at Lucy. "Lucky I've got that job." Then he saw Father's face. "Well, I took it to show Jerry, and he had to go to the priest's house for confession, and I waited on the priest's front porch, and then we went to the station to watch the train come in, and then—"

"Amory! Come to the point!" Father bellowed.

"Well, when we got back here, I reached in my pocket to show Lucy that her fancy box wasn't so safe after all, and my pocket was empty. And there was a hole in it, too, and Mother, you really should mend all my pockets," Amory said severely.

"Don't you go trying to blame your mother," Father scolded, "or I'll truly lose my temper. And the first five dollars you earn, I'll have the Langdon bank change to a five-dollar gold piece for Lucy. Sometimes I think you need confession more than Jerry does." At that, Father began to calm down, talking to Amory, very seriously.

"There aren't any pluses for anybody in all this, but I am glad, Amory, that you had the decency to confess before anyone else got the blame." Then Father began to boil again. "And Lucy, I don't want you storming around the village accusing people of crimes. Just see how far off you would have been."

Amory heard Mr. Schneider say "WHOA" to his team, out in front of the house. In a split second, he picked up his package of clean clothes, gave Mother a pecking kiss, said good-bye to Father and Lucy, and dashed out the door.

"He's lucky," Lucy said to Mother. "He can always get out of trouble, and I can't." Then she thought of Nora and Nora's troubles, and she wondered how Nora felt about that hired man. Did she like him now or hate him? And was she afraid for herself and her baby?

The more she thought of Nora, the more she understood that there was a lot more to be afraid of, a lot more bad luck and trouble than she'd ever known about.

An Elevator Burns

The next day Father had to drive to Langdon. "You'd better come with me, Caroline, and see Dr. Stewart. Dr. Carmer isn't back, and you need an examination." Father sounded anxious, and Lucy worried even more about Mother.

"Maybe Dr. Stewart can give you some medicine so you won't have to lie down so much," she said. "You're not the way you used to be."

"I don't think you need to worry," Mother replied, "but I should go. Only I don't like to take you to Langdon now, Lucy. There's infantile paralysis there. Could you stay here?"

"Have the Owens over to keep you company," Father suggested. "We'll take your rolls of film to the Opie Studio. How's that for a reward?"

"With Amory on the farm, the cookie jar is full. Have a party in the stone house. Much better than being exposed to infantile germs. Around Wales, it seems safe this year."

So right after dinner, Mother and Father dressed for an afternoon in Langdon. Father even blacked his high shoes, and Mother wore her best hat with lavender flowers. "Since Nora's named the baby Noreen Caroline, I must buy her a baby sweater," Mother said as she kissed Lucy good-bye.

After they had gone, Lucy set out the tea things on the table in the stone house. But when she went indoors for the cookies and milk, Gwen phoned.

"We were all coming over this afternoon, but now Papa says we've got to go to Hannah with him. And we might have to stay overnight. Bother!" As minister's girls, the Owens weren't allowed to say anything stronger than *bother*, but they'd all learned to make it sound like swearing.

Lucy wanted to swear herself. She put back the cookies, after extravagantly giving Topsy three whole cookies in a row. "Sometimes you're my only friend, Topsy," she muttered.

About five in the afternoon, Lucy began to look along the road for the folks. The phone rang. The operator said, "Long distance for the Johnstons."

"I'm the only Johnston here. I'm Lucy," she answered.

Mother's voice came over the wire, but she sounded as far away as Grand Forks. "Glad to know you're Lucy," Mother joked. Then she said seriously, "The Regal has broken down. We're at a garage and may not be home until after dark."

"But you will come home tonight, won't you?"

Lucy asked. She hated being alone in the house after it was pitch dark.

"Oh, yes. You just stay with the Owens, and we'll pick you up when we get home. The three minutes are up. Don't you worry about me or anything else. Only the Regal is in trouble." And Mother hung up, before Lucy could say that the Owens were away.

Lucy made her own supper, mostly more cookies and milk. Then she sat on the front porch, holding Topsy. She had read until she was tired of books, so she sat dreaming of her snapshots, wondering whether any of her pictures would be any good.

When it was nearly dark, she heard a horse and buggy stop in front of the house. Carrying Topsy, she stepped off the porch and saw it was Mr. Smith and Roger.

"I was looking for your ma. Mrs. Smith left her sweater here on the day of the Aid. Told her I'd fetch it for her."

"Just wait a moment. It's upstairs," and Lucy ran quickly through the dark for the sweater and then out to the road with it. All the time she held Topsy, and since Topsy came from the Smith farm originally, both Roger and Mr. Smith had to pat her.

"Her brothers aren't anything compared to her," Roger said. "Your father bought the smallest, but she's the smartest. If you ever want to sell her back—"

"Never!" Lucy broke in.

Roger laughed. "That's the way I'd feel too." They left at a speedy trot, and Lucy seemed more alone than before. But she daydreamed for a little about Roger. He was one boy she liked.

She went to the kitchen now to light a lamp, but before it was lit, she heard a man come pounding along the back walk, calling, "Mr. Johnston, Mr. Johnston!" Lucy hurried through the shed to find Mr. Butler at the back door, out of breath and very sweaty.

"I want for your pa to see me—" He swallowed and started over. "I mean I want to see your pa, now! Can I talk to your pa, here, right now?" He looked scared, and he was shaking.

"My father's not here. He's in Langdon." Lucy was going to add that he'd be home soon, but Mr. Butler didn't wait. He bolted, and was gone.

Suddenly bells began ringing: the Catholic church bell, then the Methodist one, and finally the school bell clanged with the others. A fire! It must be a fire. Lucy began to shiver, though it wasn't cold. She remembered far too well the raging fire last winter when nearly all of Main Street burned.

She dumped Topsy into her basket and ran out the back door. From there she could hear the bells more clearly than in the kitchen, but she couldn't see any flames or even any smoke. There was a wind, but it wasn't blowing from the village toward her house.

Into the house and up the stairs to the back bedroom window she ran, her breath coming in little catches. For a moment she saw no more from the upstairs window than she had from the back door.

Then a long flame leaped toward the sky from the first grain elevator across the railroad tracks. Then another orange flame flared upward and then another and another. Now the whole great wooden building was a tower of flames, fanned by the wind.

She pushed up the window and heard the crackling and roar of the blaze. The bells tolled on, and men shouted as they came rushing out of their houses to sprint toward the fire.

At first she thought only of the danger to Main Street and the houses on that side of town. Then she thought of the other five elevators, all empty until the grain was harvested. How did an empty elevator catch on fire? Spontaneous combustion was a danger when the dusty grain came in, but how could a fire start in August?

No matter how it began, the fire was raging now, with the wind blowing toward the other two elevators on that side of the crossing. For a split second, she thought of going to Dickermans' or to Kinsers', but she knew that wouldn't be right. When Wales had a fire, you stayed by your house to guard it.

So she went down to sit on the back steps, with Topsy for company. The wind whipped the flames higher and higher, until they met the black sky and seemed also to clutch at the next elevator. Lucy's great fear, however, was that at any moment the wind might shift and blow sparks and flames toward her own house.

She fixed her eyes on the billowing flames, and she listened to the nagging bells that called people from all over the countryside to come help the village, though she knew nobody could stop an elevator fire. Last winter a bucket brigade had saved most of the village stores, but buckets were almost funny when you saw the height of an elevator. At least this was early dark and not so scary as a middle-of-the-night fire.

After a time, she could see that the flames were blowing less violently. The wind must be dying down a little. She stood up and walked around the back-yard, wetting her finger and holding it high above

her head to test the wind. It was still blowing away from their house. And it was not blowing very hard, more like a breeze than a Dakota wind.

Then along the walk came Mrs. Flint, dragging Dorrie with one hand and pulling Morrie along with the other. She looked terrified. Her hair was flying, and she was crying and so was Morrie. Dorrie, of course, wasn't crying. She was bellowing.

"What does your mother say? Should I get things out of my house or leave them to burn?" Mrs. Flint called and cried at the same time. "And Mr. Flint's away for a couple of days, and what a time to abandon me, and the whole town will burn to a crisp, won't it?"

Since she continued to weep while she talked, Mrs. Flint's speech wasn't clear about anything. But she

was very clear about her fears, and Lucy saw Mrs. Flint in a new way. She was a grown woman, but she was even more afraid of things than Lucy was.

"Mother and Father are on their way home from Langdon," Lucy explained over Dorrie's howls. "But the houses are safe, Mrs. Flint, as long as the wind doesn't blow our way. Do you want to come in?"

When Mrs. Flint hesitated, Morrie stopped crying, so Lucy spoke to him. "Wet your finger, Morrie, and hold it as high as you can. Now, which side feels the wind?"

"Not much wind at all," he reported as he repeatedly wet his finger and tested the air, first from one spot in the yard and then another.

Quickly Lucy sucked her finger and held it high. Sure enough—the wind had died down entirely.

"Mrs. Flint, the fire can't possibly burn down your

house now or anybody's house," Lucy assured her.

"I suppose," said Mrs. Flint, as both she and Dorrie stood looking at Lucy, "you might really know. You're not very old, but you've lived all your life in this godforsaken village." Mrs. Flint then put her hand up to her hair, and she must have felt how frazzled she looked.

"Come along, darlings," she said. "We'll go home and close all the windows and the doors and go upstairs to bed. Nothing can hurt us there."

"Shutting up the house isn't a very good way to escape a—" Lucy began. Mrs. Flint's eyes opened very wide again, and Dorrie began to moan. Instead of finishing the sentence with the word *fire*, Lucy said, "The worst of the fire is over. If you want to talk to my folks, they'll soon be here."

Mrs. Flint only nodded in reply and turned to go home, Morrie now running ahead, but Dorrie sobbing and clutching her mother's skirt.

As Lucy watched them go, she decided that to grow up and be as old as Mrs. Flint and still be afraid of everything wouldn't really be growing up at all.

She took Topsy inside, lit a lamp, and sat down to read the last *Saint Nicholas* magazine, waiting for the folks.

Before long she heard the Regal's honking horn, and she ran out to open the front gate. Mother got out at once, but Father left the engine running and called, "What's on fire? We saw the blaze way across the prairie."

"It's one of the elevators, Father. And if the wind hadn't died down, all three on that side of the crossing would have gone. What a fire!"

"Open the barn door, Lucy. I'll put the Regal away

and walk down. You go to bed, Caroline. It's been a long day for you." Then as Lucy moved toward the barn, she overheard him say, "Strange for an empty elevator to burn down."

"Were you at the Owens'?" Mother asked, when she and Lucy were in the house together.

"No, they had to go to that miserable Hannah church again. But, Mother, Mrs. Flint came over and she was so scared that she was crying. She looked almost scared to death. Honest, she did."

"You must have been scared too, Lucy—all alone when an elevator burns! I'd have been terribly frightened," Mother said as she took off her hat and coat.

"Are you afraid of fires? Do you get goose pimples all over you when you see a building burn?" Lucy asked in amazement. She recalled that last winter when the whole town had been threatened by fire, Mother had been very calm.

"Of course I'm afraid of fires. I always was, but here in Wales, with not enough water, no firemen, and no fire engine, I'm worse than afraid—I'm petrified," Mother confessed. "But I never let you children see how scared I am. What's the use? And there's usually something that has to be done. So I do it."

Mother looked down at Lucy and smiled. "Perhaps what needs to be done right now is give you a hug and go up to bed."

And Lucy returned the hug by throwing her arms around Mother, not only because she was glad the folks were home but because it was a comfort to know Mother could have fears too, without being a Mrs. Flint.

The next morning Lucy hurried down to the tracks

to take a picture of the remains of the elevator. She carefully took snaps from all four sides, but she knew the pictures wouldn't amount to much—nothing but a heap of charred wood, a few pieces of twisted metal, and one iron pipe that stuck up several feet in the air.

How could such a looming high building, one of the six towers that had always marked her village on the horizon, be so demolished, so utterly gone?

Since it was a Saturday morning, the crowd of children standing around the elevator ruins included boys and girls from the country one-room schools as well as all the children in Wales. So Lucy was not surprised to see Mary Hoffer and her oldest brother, Tim, drive up in the red Maxwell runabout auto that the Hoffers had bought from Father when he got his Regal.

"Hello," called Tim as he came toward Lucy. "Had a big fire, didn't you? A city like Wales always does things in a big way," he joked. Lucy was shy with him because he was so handsome—with black, curly hair and big blue eyes—but she also felt she knew him because he drove the auto she had so often ridden in.

With Mary, though she had not seen her often, Lucy always felt at home. Mary was somehow both a girl and a woman, especially now that she taught school. "Your father has promised to come out and visit my school before the end of the season, Lucy. Why don't you come too?" Mary invited her. "I won't try to teach you anything, but I'd like to show you my children—all fourteen of them." Mary smiled proudly.

"Talks like a mother of fourteen," Tim teased. "And a couple of them are taller than she is!"

"The tallest ones are working in the fields now, and you'll see only the little ones, Lucy," Mary said. "Come if you can, won't you?" And she said it so that Lucy at once decided she'd go.

Later at dinner she discussed it with Father. "Tim teased Mary because she called them her children, but I liked that," Lucy said.

"That's why I'm sure she's a born teacher," Father replied. "I wouldn't give two cents for a teacher who wasn't fond of her pupils. When we go to her school, why don't you take Topsy and have her waltz in her new outfit to entertain the youngsters?" he suggested.

"You sound like a traveling circus, instead of a school inspector," Mother said. "Need me to join the show and play the waltz for Topsy?"

"About Topsy, Father," Lucy asked seriously, "is it safe in a country school when distemper is around?"

"There won't be a dog at school," Father said. Then he laughed. "You're thinking of 'Mary Had a Little Lamb,' and your Topsy's no lamb." He reached under the table to give Topsy a bite of cheese. "That dog! Sometimes I think she's put a spell on us so we'll spoil her." Father spoke crossly. This time he'd broken the rule about feeding a dog at the table, and he wanted to make it seem Topsy's fault.

"You blame everything on a spell," Lucy said. "Maybe you just made up my spell, and the northern lights aren't special at all."

"Hand me that thick brown book from the bottom shelf, and I'll show you something about the lights," he replied. He opened it to a bookmark, passed it to Lucy, and she read: "The Finns believe the northern lights are fires kept burning by a god to show travelers the way in winter."

"How about that? It may not be a spell, but it's taking care of people, isn't it?" Father asked. "You may like the next bit of folklore even better."

So next, Lucy read: "In Estonia the northern lights are said to be a wedding in the sky, attended by guests whose sledges and horses emit the radiance."

"A wedding in the sky," Lucy repeated. "I do like that—better than Amory's old shotgun wedding," she added.

"Don't worry too much about Nora," Mother said softly. "She'll be all right, especially since they're all moving away this winter."

"I forgot to tell you, Father, that Mr. Butler came running here to see you, just before the elevator burst into flames. He was so excited, he said first, 'I want your pa to see me,' and then he said it the right way, 'I want to see your pa.'" Lucy giggled. "He really was mixed up, wasn't he?"

"Hmmmm," said Father, looking at Mother. "A slip of the tongue is a strange thing."

Blood
Poisoning

~~～ 9e ～~~

Monday afternoon was a perfect Dakota late summer day, a breeze that wasn't too gusty and a sun that wasn't too hot. Mother and Lucy were weeding the flower garden together when a wagon stopped in front of the house. Amory climbed down, said a loud thank-you, and came limping through the gate. And the wagon went on toward Main Street.

"Amory, what are you limping for?" Mother hurried toward him. "You haven't got a fever, have you? There isn't infantile paralysis on any of the farms east of town, is there? What is the matter with you anyway?"

"It's not infantile. I know that much," Amory answered. "But it hurts like—like—" Amory's face twisted with pain, as he went up the steps to the front porch. "Well, like the devil!" he said, looking back over his shoulder at Mother to see whether she'd scold him for such language.

But Mother was far too alarmed to scold. She was right behind him and made him sit down at once on a porch chair. She untied his shoe and started to pull it off, very gently. But Amory let out a loud OUCH and pushed her away while he slowly, slowly eased the shoe off his foot. Inside the black stocking his foot was swollen fat.

Next he pulled down his stocking and peeled it, inch by inch, off his foot. The foot was a bright red, even purple in splotches, and puffy all over.

"What's wrong? What did you do to it?" Mother asked in a frightened voice.

"I didn't do anything. I just got a blister under my heel—see, kind of on the bottom of my foot. It hurt, but not too much to walk yesterday. Then today when I got up and put on the same stockings and my shoes—well, I couldn't be any use, so Mr. Schneider was coming to the store and he brought me."

"Good thing that Dr. Carmer's back in town," Mother spoke rapidly. "Sit there, and I'll phone to see if he can come."

"Yah, he's probably drunk when I'm here dying," Amory said.

Mother paid no attention. She went right to the dining room, turned the little black handle on the wall phone, and asked central to give her Dr. Carmer's office. On the porch, the children heard her say, "This is Mrs. Johnston. Amory's got an awful-looking foot. I'm afraid it's blood poisoning. Can you come right away?" Dr. Carmer must have answered *yes*, because

Mother said, "That's good. We'll look for you." And she hung up.

Mother hurried back to Amory. "He's coming immediately. We won't bother to get you upstairs. Lucy and I'll help you into the kitchen. There we'll clean you up a bit, and I'll boil some water. He may need it and—"

"Boiling water!" Amory exclaimed. "You're not getting ready to cook me!"

"It's no joke, Amory," Mother said impatiently. But Lucy could tell that Mother wasn't really cross, only so upset that she couldn't take a joke.

"I don't understand how infection could have come so quickly," Mother said. "Only a blister yesterday, and now such a ghastly foot." She seemed to be talking to herself.

Then she began to organize for the emergency. "Run upstairs, Lucy, and bring down some clean bath towels and the white china basin from my room—yes, and two white linen towels, one for the doctor to wipe his hands on and one to cover the end of the kitchen table so he can spread out the things he may need."

Mother was already busily scrubbing Amory's face and hands in the tin kitchen basin. "How come you scrub my face and hands? It's only my foot that the doctor is coming to see," Amory complained.

"Well, he can't avoid seeing your face and hands, too," Mother sputtered, as she looked out the window again to watch for the doctor.

"Here comes Dr. Carmer, Lucy. You catch him at the back door and tell him to come in this way—it's the quickest." Mother gave Amory's face a last swipe with the towel and dumped the tin basin of soapy water.

Lucy scooted through the shed and held the back screen door wide open as she called to Dr. Carmer, "Mother says to come in this way. Amory's in the kitchen."

As Dr. Carmer came toward her, Lucy realized why people said he was the handsomest man in town. He was tall and had shiny black hair, big brown eyes, and a dark, clipped moustache. Mother and Father never mentioned his being handsome, but they both agreed he was a very good doctor. So good that he'd never be in Wales if it weren't for what they called his "drinking problem."

Now he came in past Lucy, looking very serious and carrying his polished black leather bag. "I hope you're well, Lucy," he said as he went in. She understood that he didn't want to talk, so she only replied, "Hello, Dr. Carmer," and ushered him to the front room, after he had spoken to Mother.

In the living room he took off his suit jacket, rolled up his extremely white shirt-sleeves almost to his shoulders, and coming again to the kitchen, asked Lucy to fix warm water in the china basin while he put out his instruments on the kitchen table. Finally he took soap from his bag and washed his hands; over and over again he soaped. That was another point Mother always made in his favor. "He's very clean," she always said. "Everything about him is immaculate."

Mother and Lucy and Amory had intently watched all the preparations. Now the doctor lifted Amory's leg so that he could inspect the bottom of his foot. Amory winced and let out a moaning *Ohhhhh.*

"Began with a blister? And you wore this black stocking on it for a day or two?" Dr. Carmer asked.

"Yes, it was covered, so I didn't think it could get infected," Amory answered. "But now it hurts—really hurts—all along my foot and up above my ankle too."

"I can see that it must," Dr. Carmer said. Then he spoke to Mother. "I don't want to alarm you, Mrs. Johnston, but he's got a good start on a case of blood poisoning unless we can stop it here. See those lines above his ankle? That's where the infection is already spreading." He picked up a sharp instrument that made Lucy shudder.

"I've got to do some drastic cleansing," the doctor continued to Mother. "Can you hold his leg steady while I work? And Amory, I won't lie to you. This will be a bad few minutes for you." And the doctor began to scrape and probe.

Lucy retreated to the door into the living room, but she didn't go through the door. She stood with her eyes closed, for she didn't want to watch and yet she did want to watch. So she stayed there, knowing that the doctor must be hurting Amory, but not hearing more than a repeated "Ouw, ow, ouch!" She had to admit to herself that Amory was much braver about pain than she ever was. She'd have cried and even yelped.

Then the doctor spoke to Lucy, and she opened her eyes fast. "Lucy, your mother is fainting. Draw up that other chair for her to sit on and see that she puts her head down on her lap." To Mother he said, "I can't stop now, Mrs. Johnston. You'll be all right in a minute."

Lucy eased Mother into the chair and bent her head

forward. But Mother was so limp she almost fell all
the way forward onto the floor. Swiftly Lucy pulled
the sliding breadboard partway out of the kitchen cab-
inet, and Mother laid her head on that.

Then the doctor spoke sharply to Lucy once more.
"Come here. I need you. Hold your brother's leg up
like this," and he demonstrated how it should be done.
"I've got to cut a little deeper."

Lucy grabbed Amory's leg, and instead of watching the doctor's knife, she stared at Amory's white

face. As she stared, Amory's eyes closed, his head fell back, and he went limp all over—as limp as Mother.

"Another Johnston knocked out," Dr. Carmer announced calmly. "I'm nearly done, Lucy. Please hang onto your senses until I finish. Look out the window if you like, but grip that whole foot and hold it steady."

In a couple of minutes he told her, "Now you can look. The worst is over. I'm putting on the bandage." He was wrapping yards of gauze around Amory's foot until it was the size of a small pumpkin.

Amory came out of his faint just in time to hear Dr. Carmer say, "There'll be no walking on that foot for a week."

"A whole week? Is that what you said?" Amory asked in a fuzzy voice. Dr. Carmer just kept on wrapping the foot, and Amory began to plan. "Maybe I could go to Main Street on crutches. I'll bet people would be surprised to see me on crutches."

"There isn't a pair of crutches your size in the whole village," Dr. Carmer said. "You're to stay right here at home, and I'll come every day to dress the wound and to make sure you're not out rambling all over town. Later, perhaps, you can use a cane."

"I'll use the cane on him if he tries to leave the house," Mother threatened in a feeble whisper, as she lifted her head from the breadboard and gazed at the huge bandaged foot.

"Oh, you've recovered? You surprised me, Mrs. Johnston. You're not the fainting kind," Dr. Carmer said. Then he joked with Lucy. "The only Johnston to keep her wits, weren't you? Ever think of becoming a nurse?"

"No, no, never!" Lucy replied emphatically. "I'm afraid when I see people bleed or know they're getting hurt."

"I thought so. That's why I had you look out the window. I couldn't have you passing out, too."

After he had thoroughly washed his hands again and repacked his black bag, he said to Mother, "I should warn you about something. Boil all the children's black stockings before they wear them the first time. That way they'll be safe. Because of the war, black dye that used to come from Germany is made here now, with a substitute that can be poisonous if it gets into the body. This isn't the first case I've seen lately."

"My mother put poisonous stockings on me!" Amory exclaimed.

"Amory, don't make me sound like a witch," Mother begged, as she stood up a little shakily. "Dr. Carmer, I don't know what we would have done if you hadn't been here. I'm so glad you are back from your—" Mother stopped. Lucy and Amory and the doctor too knew she stopped because she didn't want to say "from your cure for drinking too much."

"Keep his foot up, propped on a chair," Dr. Carmer said, paying no attention to Mother's pause. "Amory, you can tell your father you behaved like a soldier. Lucy, you can tell your father that you saved the day. And Mrs. Johnston, I don't know what you should tell your husband except that you may need more rest."

"Rest! All I do lately is rest," complained Mother.

"That's true," Lucy agreed. She'd never seen Mother lie down as much as she had in the weeks since their Minnesota trip. And no one had said anything about the results of Mother's visit to Dr. Stewart. It was all very troubling.

Mother showed Dr. Carmer out and then collapsed in her rocking chair. "What a scare you've given me, Amory," she said wearily. "But your father will be proud of your taking it like a man. When he comes home, he'll go up in the barn loft and get your grandfather's canes."

"Canes!" howled Amory. "You poison me and I might die or lose a leg or a foot, and you want me to go around with a cane? I got to have crutches. No point in being half-dead unless people know it," he argued.

"I don't like to scold you after all you've been through, but you are the world's original show-off." Then Mother saw the disappointment on Amory's face. "Never mind, dear," she hastened to say, "since there are no crutches for you in Wales, perhaps your father can make some."

Amory looked so pleased that she glimpsed what he was planning. "But you're not going out of this house, you know—no parading along Main Street with crutches," she said severely.

Amory's face fell. But soon after Lucy and Mother had helped him to the living room, he was happy again, ordering Lucy about. "Lucy, how about your running upstairs for my book on the Civil War— might be under my pillow still, might be on the third shelf in the red bookcase, might be—anyway, you find it. And while you're there, bring down my Erector set, the set of checkers, the Parcheesi box, and—oh, yes, maybe I can practice with rubber darts on my target, and there's that new battle map of Europe— I've got to keep track of how the war's going in—"

"Amory!" Lucy finally got in a word. "I can't possibly remember all that, and I couldn't lug it all, even if I did."

"Well, you'll just have to make several trips," Amory told her, very matter of fact. "And I want you to phone Jerry and tell him about me—no, don't tell him. Just ask him to come so I can tell him." Lucy opened her mouth to object again, but Amory had thought of food. "And I'm really hungry after all this doctor-business, so how about a half-dozen cookies— no, better bring the whole cookie jar and put it here beside me," and he motioned to the sofa, where he was lying.

Mother had something to say at that. "You're using Lucy as messenger, entertainer, and—"

"And slave," Lucy growled. She saw the days ahead filled with errands for Amory as well as the extra errands she was doing for Mother, and her legs grew tired.

Then she felt mean. "After all," she told herself, "Amory was much braver than I could have been." And she climbed the stairs to Amory's room, counting on her fingers all the things he wanted. In three trips she had everything piled around him, the map hanging on the bookcase key and the dartboard across the room. Then she had to sit and play game after game of checkers, with Amory always winning.

That night Father came home tired, but he went out to his tool kit in the barn to nail together a pair of crutches. By the time Mother had heavily padded the underarm crosspieces, they were so wide that Amory complained.

"Look! They cut into me, under my arms. Like as not I'll lose both arms now as well as my foot or maybe my leg. Doesn't anybody in this family have any pity on me?" he wailed.

So Father dragged the crutches out to the barn to make them over. And Mother shook her head and said, "How could you be so brave and uncomplaining this afternoon, and so cantankerous now?"

Amory put on a sad look and smiled a saintly smile. "I suppose it's because being a bedridden invalid is so much harder to bear," he sighed.

"You're not bedridden—only chair-ridden," Lucy corrected him.

Then Mother began to defend Amory. "It is hard for him, Lucy, to sit still all afternoon and then to-morrow and tomorrow after that."

Lucy started to say, "And don't forget me—I'm running my legs off for him," but she knew she'd get no sympathy for that.

The next morning Lucy was delighted to welcome Jerry. Amory gave a demonstration of his crutches, and then they spent hours playing games and building with Amory's Erector set. Lucy scuttled out of sight as soon as she could, and she stayed out at the stone house until dinnertime, discussing with the Owen girls what the four new teachers might be like.

Last year the one man, Mr. Donner, who had taught the ninth- and tenth-grade room, had married Lucy's teacher. So this year the girls felt that the new man must marry one of the three women teachers, and the possibilities were endless.

The Firebug

At suppertime that evening Father had a call to go out in the country and draw up a will for Mr. Schlegel, who was very ill.

"Come with me, Caroline," Father said as he took out of his desk the papers he needed. "You've been guarding your son so closely these last twenty-four hours that you haven't even seen as far as the fence around our yard."

"I'd love to—twilight's the most beautiful time on the prairie," Mother replied. "Yes—I'll go. Lucy, you take care of Amory. And Amory, you stay put," Mother ordered. Then she hurried to get ready, and soon Lucy had swung open the driveway gate and they were gone.

Lucy slammed the gate and went slowly through

the porch and into the house. A drive in the country wasn't very exciting, but neither was it very exciting to play checkers all evening with Amory and be beaten every game.

After an hour, Amory was hungry. "While I check the war news in today's paper so we can put pins in the right places on my map, you make me two—no, three or four peanut butter sandwiches," he instructed Lucy. "Put jelly in them, too."

So Lucy handed him the *Grand Forks Herald* and went to make sandwiches. It was getting dark, and she lit the kerosene lamp. She got out the bread, the butter from the crock in the shed, the jelly and peanut butter from the kitchen shelf. But she never made the sandwiches.

As she passed the back kitchen window, she looked out. And suddenly she saw a burst of flame from one of the two elevators left standing on the south side of the crossing. In a minute, first the two church bells and then the school bell began their dismal *ding-dong*, just as they had four nights before.

It was all so like that first fire that for a second she thought she must be dreaming. But Amory wasn't dreaming.

"What's going on?" he shouted from the living room. "Hand me my crutches! Sounds like a fire! My crutches! I'm not sitting in here while the whole town burns down."

"You won't believe it, Amory. It's another elevator fire!"

"I do believe it," he echoed. "I missed the last one and I'm not going to miss this one, too." And before she could get to the living room, he had hobbled to the kitchen window. "Wow! Nothing like an elevator to make a bonfire!" Amory yelled almost happily.

Lucy left the window and ran outdoors to check the wind. There wasn't a breath stirring this time. Poor Wales, in four days it was being cut from a six-elevator town to a four-elevator village, unless the other one on the south side also caught fire. Then there'd be only three.

"Open the screen door. I'm coming out," Amory called. Lucy helped him hop to the backyard. "Now I need a chair," he said. So Lucy ran in and brought out a straight chair. "And I forgot—a stool for my foot," Amory specified. So Lucy brought that. She plunked it down in front of him.

"There now," Lucy said, "that's all. I'm not bringing you another thing. I want to watch the fire." She stood leaning on his chair, glad that this time she was not alone, though in the windless air, this fire was not as frightening as the last one.

They could hear the crackling of the flames and the shouts of the men as the flames went higher and higher into the darkening sky. But this time the flames went straight up, a threat to the one elevator next to the burning one, but no threat to any house in the village.

"There was an emperor who sat and watched Rome burn," Amory began. "I feel a little like him, only I'm hungry. Where are those sandwiches? I'll bet that emperor had a feast while the city burned."

"You're not an emperor, and I'm not your slave. No sandwiches while an elevator burns!" Lucy refused to budge.

Then through the back gate came the three Flints: Dorrie screaming, Morrie big-eyed and frightened, and Mrs. Flint shouting at the top of her lungs,

"What about this fire? Do your folks think this one will spread?"

Lucy felt it was Amory's turn to deal with the Flints. "Our folks aren't home, Mrs. Flint, but I'm here, and I can assure you there is no danger," he yelled, in order to be heard over Dorrie. Mrs. Flint was calmed more by Amory than she had been by Lucy. He spoke with such authority that he seemed an expert on elevator fires, though this was the first one he'd ever seen.

Mrs. Flint looked down at Amory's swathed foot. "You poor little boy! Did your folks go away and leave you here, and now there's this terrible conflagration and—"

Amory interrupted her. "Don't you worry, Mrs. Flint. My folks trust me, and I'm taking care of my little sister."

Lucy was about to say, "My folks left me to take care of him," but it was no use arguing with Amory, especially when an elevator was burning and Dorrie Flint was howling.

"Do you want to stay?" Amory invited them. "Lucy would be glad to carry out three chairs, and we could all watch the fire."

"What a polite boy. You've improved since your trip to the city, haven't you?" Mrs. Flint smiled at him. Then she seemed suddenly to remember the fire. "Look!" she cried out. "The walls are falling!"

Amory snatched his crutches and stood for a better view. Lucy ran to the well platform, turned over the high, empty tub, and climbed on it. There she saw that Mrs. Flint was right. The elevator walls spread outward like the opening petals of an enormous orange tulip. And then with a deafening crash the walls fell, and the fire was flattened.

Dorrie held her breath after the crash. But she turned and took off for home so fast that Mrs. Flint had to run top speed to catch up. Morrie gave a last look at Amory's bandaged foot, and then he was gone also.

At that moment, the Regal honked, and Lucy ran to the front to let the folks drive into the yard. Mother and Father said at once, "Which elevator is it this time?" And Father added, "We saw it miles away."

"Were you badly frightened?" Mother asked.

"Why, no, I wasn't," Lucy answered honestly. And she asked herself, "Was it because Amory was here, or am I getting over my fears—my spell changing me, perhaps?"

"I would have been scared stiff," Mother admitted. "You're getting ahead of me, Lucy."

The next morning Jerry brought Amory all the village gossip about the fire. At dinner Amory shared the gossip. "Everybody says there must be a firebug in Wales—a real arsonist. Imagine that—in Wales! Somebody in town is burning buildings. And everybody's guessing who it is and how we can catch him and—"

"Hold on, Amory," Father interrupted. "There's too much talk in this village this morning about arson. Every single person who came into the bank this morning suggested that these two elevator fires were set, and everybody's got a different idea of who did it."

"But how can we ever be safe if there's somebody loose setting buildings afire?" Lucy was alarmed.

"Now both you children listen to me," Father commanded. He waited until they were both looking at him before he went on. "Arson is a very serious charge. A man can be sent to prison for it. All this guessing can't prove anything, and it might hurt some innocent person. I don't insure any Wales elevators, so it's not my business—and it's certainly not your business, either."

"But don't you think it's very suspicious?" Amory pressed on. "First one burns down, and then four nights later this other one bursts into flame. And the first time there was a wind blowing toward the one that burned last night. But the wind died down before the whole row caught fire."

Even Father couldn't stop Amory this time. "And if that wind hadn't died down—well, Jerry says people think somebody wanted to burn this one before, but his scheme didn't work the first time, so he had to set fire to it."

"Amory, you're just repeating what Jerry has heard. You don't know a single thing definitely, do you?" Father asked.

Amory shifted his argument. "Well, who'd want to burn an empty elevator, anyway?"

"An arsonist burns building just to see them burn, doesn't he? Isn't it a kind of insanity?" Mother questioned.

"What was burned—no grain, nothing but that tall, empty elevator," Lucy said.

"The elevator and the account books," Father said, and then abruptly stopped. "You're going to hear a lot of gossip, so I might as well tell you that it's possible there was some record in the books—of grain a farmer had sold that hadn't belonged to him, of money the elevator man had loaned to a farmer or had given to someone else. Who knows? And maybe the fire wasn't set at all. Buildings in this town can burn without being set. We know that." He spoke so severely that no one said anything in reply.

"Now how about another dish of that chocolate pudding?" Father said, passing his empty dish to Mother.

Everyone concentrated on second helpings of chocolate pudding and heavy cream, until Lucy thought she could risk one more question about the elevators.

"Will they rebuild the two elevators that burned?" she asked, watching Father closely to be sure he wouldn't bark at her. Father could be very grumpy when he didn't want to talk.

"I've been wondering the same thing," Mother said.

"No, Wales will never again have six elevators," Father answered. "With the Sarles branch to the west of us finished, not so much grain is hauled to Wales. Remember, Caroline, the first fall we were here, how the wagons heaped with grain were lined up along Main Street and out past the last house in the village, all waiting a turn to deliver wheat to the elevators? Those days are gone."

"So now Wales isn't much, is it?" Lucy asked dolefully. "Almost any old North Dakota village has three or four elevators, and I was so proud that Wales had six."

"Yes, they did make a nice showing along the horizon," Mother said. "But, Harry, are the two men who ran those elevators out of a job? What a pity! Both the Torsens and the Logans went to our church, and Sam Logan was the only tenor in the choir."

"They'll have to move somewhere else," Father

said. "Too bad, because if there was skulduggery, they may get the tarnished reputations and not someone else who might be—" Father realized suddenly that he was talking about something he'd forbidden the family to speak of. He changed the subject.

"War news is bad—very bad. Did you see when you put pins in your map of the Western Front last night, Amory, that the armies aren't moving? Just standing still and slaughtering each other in the mud."

"Will one side ever win?" Mother asked gravely.

"Probably not until the USA goes in—on the side of England and France, of course," Father said.

"But Woodrow Wilson might get reelected president, just because he's kept us out of the war—that's what the election posters say," Lucy reminded him. "Have we got to go to war?"

"Can't keep us out forever—nobody can," Father said angrily. "That's why I won't vote for Wilson in November. He's only dreaming. I'm voting for Hughes."

The idea that her country might soon be in the war startled Lucy. "But, Father, wouldn't it be better if we didn't have to go to the war?" she began.

He looked at her and said, "Of course, Lucy, but sometimes bad things have to happen, and it's best to be prepared . . . But enough of that. Let me tell you about your new teachers. The school board has had a real problem in hiring, you know—the war in Europe has opened up new jobs here, too, so not many teachers apply now. And Wales has to take whoever will come. But I do think—"

"Do you know their names, Father?" Lucy broke in. Names were always of interest to Lucy.

"Where do they come from, Harry? Used to little

villages, I hope," Mother said. "And some of them can sing in our choir, perhaps?"

Father laughed. "I don't know that they were tested for singing, but I have heard that three of them are Catholic—Mr. Grady, a Miss Laura Baxter, who is on her first job, and a Mrs. Helen O'Neil, a widow with a little girl. That leaves you only the one the school board hired as a last resort—a Miss Hortense Fothergill. She'll be teaching your room, Lucy, the seventh and eighth grades. She's not young—retires after this year."

"Hortense Fothergill—what a beautiful name!" Lucy exclaimed.

"There goes Roaring Boring again," Amory teased. "I'm glad I've got plain Mr. Grady. You can have your dense Hortense, though when she hears you've got a spell on you, she'll probably try to palm you off on—"

"I'm going to the bank for a little peace," Father said, getting up from his chair. "The food on our table is always good, Caroline, but I can't always say as much for the table conversation." And he kissed Mother and left.

"I forgot to tell you," Amory said to Mother. "Jerry says the Smith kid—those Mort Smiths who sold us this yammering Topsy—their Roger's down with infantile." Amory paused. "Got it bad."

"Infantile! Oh, no, how awful!" Mother spoke in a shocked tone. "It's their only boy—about fourteen. Why Amory, he's about your age. I must call Mrs. Sanderson. She always knows all the medical news. I sometimes wonder how long we can be lucky about such things." And Mother set about clearing the table, murmuring to herself, "Oh, dear, oh dear, some people have such bad, bad luck."

Lucy's fear of a firebug in Wales was now forgotten in her concern for Roger. Even if he didn't die, he'd be a cripple. That's what infantile did. And there was no cure. What would it be like to have that happen to you?

A One-Room
School
and A Cook Car

~~~~~ 9e ~~~~~

"Be at the big gate at ten this morning," Father said to Lucy on the day they were going out to Mary Hoffer's school. "Why not use your new doll's suitcase for Topsy's finery. The little girls would like that."

"It's not really for a doll," Lucy corrected him. "It's for the wardrobe I've designed for Clarissa, and she's only my model now." Sometimes Father wasn't very bright, Lucy thought. He still thought of her as six or seven years old.

"And Amory," Father went on, "you're well enough to help your mother. You do the dishes today."

"Me?" Amory asked in a horrified tone. "I've got a sore finger. I don't think I should put it in water, and Mother doesn't like the way I do dishes. She says

I leave so much food on the plates that she's always eating yesterday's dinner with today's. And that's not really good for us, is it?" Amory look convinced by his own argument.

"Shows you need practice. And if you can't get them clean in one go, you can do them right over." Father was not convinced.

So Amory tried another tack. "Dishes are really Lucy's job."

"Stop that nonsense. Do you or don't you eat off dishes?" And when Amory did not reply, Father insisted. "Answer me, Amory."

"Of course I eat off dishes, but there's the cream pitcher, the jam dish, the pickle dish, and the platter —lots of things I don't eat off. Besides, Mother never used to need all this help."

Father began to scowl. "I get blamed sick of your arguing, Amory. Dishes are for boys as well as girls —and today they're yours. Period!" Amory opened his mouth, but he shut it before a sound came out. Lucy ran upstairs to make her bed, since Father's face looked like a thundercloud. But she, too, wondered about Mother. She seemed worse, if anything. Did Father worry, too? Was that why he was so cross?

By the time they set off together for Mary's school, however, Father was in a good mood. Drives out in the country were what Father liked far more than sitting in his bank. Also, Lucy knew he liked to have someone ride beside him, though he often drove for miles without saying anything. Today he was silent until they saw a field of flax in bloom.

He stopped the Regal for a minute at the top of a slight rise of ground and said, "Look, Lucy, and don't ever forget it. Acres and acres of bright blue! Cities have parks and botanical gardens, but they can't equal what you're looking at." Then he put the auto in gear, drove on, and said nothing more for a while, until he noticed she was looking only at Topsy, snoozing in her lap.

"It's hot today. Why don't you put Topsy in the backseat? You'll be cooler that way," he suggested.

"I don't want to wake her," Lucy answered, cuddling the terrier closer.

"Sometimes you scare me with that dog, Lucy. She's like a person to you."

"She is a person, aren't you, Topsy?" Lucy said to the sleeping dog. Topsy waggled her tail slightly and barely opened one eye and closed it.

"She is what we called her—the miracle dog. And you're right to enjoy her, but people live at least six or seven times as long as dogs, so—" But Lucy stopped listening.

By now Father was in a talkative mood. "Have you noticed all the black-eyed Susans in bloom at the side of the road? And how about that meadowlark, in matching yellow with a black V on his neck? You shouldn't take a drive like this and see only a dog," he told her impatiently.

So she did look around her, but she continued slowly to smooth Topsy's coat, thinking to herself— "Topsy's like my baby. I brought her up, and it's me she knows and not her mother-dog."

"Harumph!" Father cleared his throat. "It must be a daydreaming spell on you, but I suppose that's better than falling asleep for a hundred years. Now before we get there, reach into that bag at your feet and see what I brought."

Lucy reached into the brown shopping bag and

pulled out a big envelope with sheets of tracing paper, a sealed ink pad and a box of rubber-stamp letters and a holder to go with them, a handful of partially used pencils, brand new crayons, red and blue pencils, a jar of white paste, and underneath everything, at least a dozen all-day suckers—all colors and flavors. Lucy wanted to try one of those herself, but she saw there were just enough for Mary's pupils, plus one for Mary to suck when they had theirs.

"They'll love all this stuff a lot more than Topsy's dancing," Lucy said. "Especially the suckers!"

Looking ahead now on the straight road across the flat prairie, Lucy saw the little white one-room school with its pump and spindly flagpole in front. And at the back stood the two outhouses, one for the girls and one for the boys. As they drove up to the school-yard, Mary Hoffer was at the door, ringing a large handbell to call in the ten or eleven children from recess.

Mary welcomed Father and Lucy, saying, "Good thing you came today. My school gets smaller all the time—nearly threshing season. So I'm getting only the little tots who'd be underfoot at home. Lucky I close on Friday anyway, because I'm going to help Mrs. Towne in the cook car with the threshing rig."

Father laughed. "I'll bet you'll earn more in three weeks on that job than you have all summer teaching." Then he said seriously, "But teaching is what you're cut out for, Mary. And I've heard from May-ville Normal School that they'll accept you for this winter session, even though you don't have your high-school diploma. I sent them a list of all the books you'd borrowed from us to read this last winter, and that convinced them that you're ready to go on."

"Wonderful!" Mary's face lit up as she said it, then she changed and looked sad. "But you know, Mr. Johnston, my father won't let me go. He says he and the boys need me to take my mother's place. I go home every night from here to do the housework so I can teach in the daytime."

"Mary, I'm going past your father's farm later, and I may be able to talk him into letting you go. If he can afford to help Tim buy our old auto, he can send you to normal school." Father spoke rather fiercely. Then he smiled. "Let's go in. I don't really have to see you teach, and I can't stay long, so how about Lucy's dog putting on a show, and then I'll leave this bag of equipment for your last days of the term."

In the school, Lucy saw that most of the seats were vacant, and she also noticed that Mary had put up pictures, drawings, and cutouts so that the room was very gay. The Wales schoolrooms had tan walls and dusty blackboards with two framed brown photographs, one of Washington and one of Lincoln. Perhaps going to a one-room country school could be fun, if you had a teacher like Mary Hoffer.

Mary introduced them first, and next Topsy, as a famous dancing-dog. So as the children gathered at the front of the room, Lucy took out the satin costume, Topsy patiently allowed herself to be dressed, and then with Father and Lucy humming a waltz— both in their off-key voices—Topsy twirled in time to the music.

The children applauded, so Lucy put Topsy through her other tricks. Then they asked so many questions that she gave almost a lecture on how to train a dog. After that, Father spoke of a bunch of wildflowers in a glass of water on the teacher's desk.

"You've picked something rare, children. Did you know that's a purple coneflower? They're common in some parts of the country, but I seldom see them here. Now who picked that?" he asked in such a way that both the flower and finding it became a triumph.

A shy little girl in a brown gingham dress stood up and said, "Please, Mr. Johnston, my brother and me did."

"And they grow in sand. It was gritty between my toes," added a very small boy, who must be her brother.

"They're right about the soil," Father said to Mary.

"And I like their observing and remembering. That's the basis of intelligence." But he saw the children had their minds on the brown paper bag and not the coneflowers, so he concluded the visit with a loud, "I must be going. Good-bye to all of you!" Lucy picked up Topsy, waved the dog's front paw at the children, and said her good-bye, too.

"Now we'll drive to the Hoffer farm," Father said as they drove away from the school. "Even you can see that Mary should become a teacher—in a bigger school and for a longer season."

"But why doesn't her father want her to go to

Mayville and get a diploma?" Lucy asked. "I thought all parents liked their children to get an education."

"Well, when she's away he may have to hire somebody to take her place. Her brothers are hard workers, but it's outdoor work. I suppose none of them wants to do the housework, even in the winter when they're not so busy."

"They sound just like Amory to me!" Lucy snorted.

"Don't be so quick to judge people, Lucy. Sometimes you sound like a little old woman. But there's the farm. You sit in the auto and hold Topsy. Don't want her mixing with other dogs these days, do we? Besides," Father had stopped the Regal and was climbing out— "Well, besides, Frank Hoffer may get angry with me and yell words not good for your ears."

Father went to the back door, knocked twice, and a tall, gaunt man in overalls came out. It was Mr. Hoffer, but he wasn't at all handsome like Tim or Mary. He looked faded and old. Instead of inviting Father in, he began to talk not far from the auto. Lucy couldn't avoid hearing what he said.

At first he talked only about the good crops and the expense of getting the harvest threshed and how he'd tried to drive the Maxwell automobile but only Tim had the knack of it. To all of this, Lucy paid little attention.

Then Father said, "I just stopped by your Mary's school. Frank, that girl's a born teacher—she's a whizz at it. But until she goes to normal school, you know she can't teach anywhere in the state except in that one room."

"I don't want her going around the state. She's the

only girl I've got. I need her home. Who'll keep house?" Mr. Hoffer motioned toward the farmhouse with his thumb.

"It's only one winter, Frank. You've got the money to send her and hire somebody now and then, if you have to." Father almost begged. "Pay out some cash and send her to Mayville. You'll never be sorry. Later on she'll earn a lot more than she can in her little one-room summer school."

Mr. Hoffer stared at his heavy work shoes for a full minute. Then Lucy heard him say, "A couple of years ago a professor from the Langdon High School told me she should get more schooling, but I know his kind. His head's full of fancy ideas!" Mr. Hoffer was now looking directly at Father. "I listen to you, Mr. Johnston. You're no professor. You're a banker, so you must know what makes money. I'll let her go."

After such a long speech, he said nothing more, only shook hands with Father and went back in the house. But not before Father had shouted to him, "You'll always be glad, Frank. Tell Mary to bring in the forms, and I'll help her fill them out."

On the way home, Father sat for a long time behind the wheel, humming to himself. Then he turned to Lucy. "Of course I'm not ashamed of having been a college professor, but you heard Frank's opinion. That's why I don't tell most people."

"Yes, but I can't see why he thinks you're brighter if you're a banker and not a professor." Lucy was puzzled.

"Partly it's because I handle money instead of reading books, I suppose. I'm the same person whether you call me a banker or a professor—just the way you're the same person whether we'd named you Lucy or Aurora Borealis."

"Oh, forget that awful name—" Then she remembered her camera on the backseat. "I meant to take a picture of Mary's children," Lucy wailed.

"Eleven children all standing still at once for a snapshot? You do live in a dream world, Lucy!" And he put his hand on her knee as he said, "But I like to have you with me, even if you were born under a mysterious spell."

On Saturday afternoon when Lucy went to the bank to get the mail for Mother, Father was showing Mary out the door. "Now remember, Mary, you need the whole year, and until the crop is sold, your father may be a little short. Let me know if you need anything." Father shook Mary's hand.

Lucy saw Mary's eyes fill with tears, and for a moment it looked like a weepy good-bye. Then Mary gave him a broad smile. "Without you, I'd never have been able to go," she said. "I won't forget." And off she went to the red Maxwell, which Tim must have taught her to drive, for she cranked the auto with an expert twist, hopped in, and drove out of town.

"She wants you to come see her in the cook car after threshing has begun," Father told Lucy. "Put it on your social calendar so you don't forget."

When the day came to go to Mrs. Towne's farm to see the threshing rig and visit the cook car, Father asked Mother if she felt well enough to come, too.

"On a golden September morning like this I feel perfectly well," Mother replied. "But here comes

Sarah Lowenstein for her piano lesson. She's the only pupil I have who really loves her lesson, so I mustn't disappoint her."

As Lucy let Sarah in the door, she felt a twinge of envy. Sarah was nearly grown up, and more than that, she was beautiful, with black, curly hair and big dark eyes. And she was very talented in music, while Lucy couldn't play three bars on the piano without making a mistake.

So Lucy and Father set off again without Mother. "You watch what goes on in the cook car so you can earn some cash that way before long." Father pretended to be serious, but Lucy knew he was joking. Even Mother couldn't manage a cook car.

The cook car was hauled from farm to farm with the threshing machine. Sixteen or eighteen men sat down at the long table spread inside three times a day for enormous meals. These were prepared by the cook and her helper, along with the midmorning and midafternoon lunches taken out to the fields.

Father loved the threshing season, especially when the crop was good; and Lucy, too, could feel the excitement as they drove into the field beside the rig. But she stood a few yards away from the huge black engine, which was attached to the tall yellow separator by a tremendous wide belt.

The noise of the thumping engine, the rattle of the grain-separator, and the shouts of the men driving racks of grain sheaves from the other fields, mixed with the fear Lucy always had of such machinery, kept her from going any closer.

She liked watching the bundles of wheat being forked into the separator and the rush of grain that poured into the wagon box to be hauled to the elevator. She even liked a little of the bellowing of the men and the jingling of the heavy horses' harness, and she enjoyed waving back to Tim Hoffer, who was the engineer's assistant. From a distance she took three snapshots of the whole rig.

But she had heard stories of the hideous accidents—of men caught in the belt or mangled by the machine, so she was glad when Father took her to the door of the cook car. It was like a small room on big wagon wheels, and both Mrs. Towne and Mary welcomed her.

"Table's not ready. Give us a hand, Lucy," Mrs. Towne called as Lucy climbed the three steps and came in the door. "Plates are piled up here. You put one at each man's place, see that each man has a knife and fork, and put these tumblers of teaspoons along the middle." Mrs. Towne was all business.

Lucy barely had the table set when she heard loud joking and the clatter of basins on the bench outside the cook car. Then in came the threshing crew, all in heavy shoes, overalls, and blue shirts and all hot, dusty, and hungry. They sat down at once, and Mrs. Towne and Mary began passing big bowls of potatoes, platters of corned beef, ham, and roast pork. Lucy helped with the vegetables—bowls of sauerkraut, beets, and carrots and mounds of mashed turnips—while Mary poured cup after cup of steaming coffee into the thick white cups, and later she passed big slabs of four kinds of pie.

Lucy kept bringing plates of bread and butter from the end of the car, but everything disappeared like snow in July. She did see some farmers and their nearly grown sons whom she knew, and to them she said hello. But most of the men were strangers. She was so busy scurrying to and fro that she didn't have time to be shy, so when one man said to Mrs. Towne, "Where'd you get the midget waitress?" Lucy felt he meant it as a compliment.

"I'm from the circus," Lucy told him, "and I'm practicing in this sideshow." It wasn't much of a joke, but all the men laughed at it.

The only man she tried not to look at was Harry Sloane. She'd known him all her life, but she'd never grown used to his having only one eye and a hole where the other one should be. He lived by himself on a farm near town, and Father said he was a genius with horses.

On the drive home, Lucy asked Father about Harry Sloane. "Didn't you tell me once that a horse kicked Harry Sloane in the eye?" she began. "But you say he's so good with horses. How did it happen?"

"Perhaps you're old enough now to learn something from it if I tell you," Father said. "Late one night Harry heard that he was going to be arrested the next day and taken to court for something he hadn't done. What scared him was that he had no proof that he hadn't done it.

"So he rushed out to his barn to hitch his horse and skip the county. But animals sense fear, and I suppose Harry was so scared that even his own horse got skittish and gave him a vicious kick. Well, that's how it happened. When he finally hitched the horse, Harry came racing to the doctor. And he never went away at all, because the next day someone else confessed."

Lucy thought a moment and then asked, "You want me to see what can happen just because someone is afraid—is that it?"

"More or less," Father answered, "though I don't

expect you to get kicked in the face trying to escape the sheriff."

Since Father was talkative, Lucy went on. "What about that firebug? Do you think he's still in Wales and will set more fires?"

"No, if those fires were set, I think they're the only ones. If a firebug is still in Wales, he must have what he wanted—cash. There's nothing else in town that he'd be paid to burn. So scratch that fear off your list. Any others left?"

"A few," Lucy replied, not wanting to tell him all the other fears that still haunted her.

Four
New Teachers

~~·~~

"Mother, I want to go to the station this afternoon to see the four new teachers come to town. May I go?"

"I don't like your hanging around that station," Mother began, when Lucy interrupted.

"We four Stone Age Girls are going together, and we're not hanging around—you make it sound awful! This is Friday, and school begins Tuesday, and I'll be the only one in the whole school who won't know which teacher is which, if I don't go to meet the train."

"All right, all right. You're beginning to argue the way Amory does," Mother complained.

Lucy bolted out the door before Mother could change her mind. At the station the girls were not alone. Every youngster in town was on the platform, waiting. And for once, the train was on time.

The first person to get off was a small, red-cheeked young woman, holding the hand of a six-year-old girl. As they stepped down, everyone heard the cheerful voice, "Here's where home is now, Polly."

"That must be the widow, Mrs. O'Neil," Lucy whispered to Gwen. "I thought widows were always old, didn't you?"

The second teacher was very young, not much older than Mary Hoffer, though she looked much more fragile than Mary. She was a rather pretty blond, but scared-looking, especially when she saw the crowd of children. "The primary room teacher, and it's her first job. Lucky she won't get any of the big pupils," Gwen said in a low voice.

No question about the third teacher. It was Mr. Grady. He handed down suitcase after suitcase to the conductor on the platform. "Polite to take care of all their bags, isn't he?" Guinevere commented.

Then Mr. Grady stepped down beside the conductor, and immediately everyone saw that he was very short. Yet he moved the bags so quickly out of the way and laughed so loud at something the conductor said that it was clear he was bursting with energy.

"Full of it, isn't he?" Gwin said so loud that both Lucy and Gwen hushed her.

There was a long pause before the last teacher appeared. Finally a very fat, white-haired woman came swaying down the three steps of the coach and slowly lowered herself to the stool the conductor had left ready for her.

She pointed back to one last bulging suitcase, and the conductor heaved that out to the platform. She buttoned her long black coat around her, and at the same time asked the conductor for something. Lucy couldn't hear the question, but the brakeman opened the door of the baggage car, jumped down, and pulled at the leash of a very fat old bulldog. The dog refused to move.

The fat teacher, who had to be Miss Hortense Fothergill, rushed toward the baggage car. "Oh, don't pull on Mr. Guggums," she cried. "He bites and he's ferocious and he's very old." She leaned far into the baggage car and encouraged Mr. Guggums to emerge. "Come on out, Guggumsy. We're here now and your lovely ride is done."

Mr. Guggums braced himself against the doorway, surveyed what he could see of Wales, and refused to budge an inch. He lifted his drooling upper lip, showed his dirty brown teeth, and growled.

The engineer leaned out of the engine cab to see what was keeping them, the conductor put away the stool, and the brakeman stood glaring impatiently at Mr. Guggums. But Miss Fothergill paid no attention to anyone but her dog. "Time to get off, Mr. Guggums," she wheedled. Mr. Guggums now turned his head and lifted his lip at her. Otherwise he was motionless.

"She's weak on discipline," Lucy muttered to Gwen, as all the schoolchildren of Wales waited for Mr. Guggums to move.

"I've got a piece of your sandwich left," Miss Fothergill coaxed. She dug into her lumpy black handbag, pulled out a mashed sandwich, removed the ham, and held it just far enough from Mr. Guggums so that he had to jump down to get it. Once out on the platform, he stood on his wide bowlegs, and Lucy gazed upon the oldest dog she'd ever seen. He was partly white, partly bald, and his eyes were a watery pink. The minute he was on the platform, the train started up, and people began to leave.

The event was over, and the four girls walked together along Main Street. Gwin was the first to speak. "Guinevere and I've got the best one, that jolly-looking Mrs. O'Neil. Edward must have that little bit of a girl-teacher, and—"

"And look what Lucy and I've got!" Gwen said morosely.

"She's kind to her dog," Lucy reminded Gwen. Then she thought of the slobbering old dog. "But what a dog!"

"When you told us her name was Miss Hortense

Fothergill, I thought she'd be beautiful," Guinevere said. "But maybe she's a good teacher, do you think?"

"She'd better be! She's got to be good at something," Lucy said, trying to forget Miss Fothergill.

The evening after the teachers arrived, Father talked about school, too. "Mr. Grady dropped into the bank, and he has good ideas for your tenth grade, Amory." Amory had skipped so many grades and was so far ahead for his age, that next year he would have to go away to school.

"But that Mr. Grady's pint-size. How can he manage the big guys like Joe Kizer when the harvest is all done and they come in?" Amory spoke contemptuously. "Bet there won't be any order."

"And my teacher," Lucy chimed in. "Did you see mine? Big as a whale."

"I don't care about the dimensions of your teachers. You forget sizes and learn. That's what school is about," Father scolded.

When Tuesday came, the four girls were going to school together. Lucy set out early for the parsonage, but after she was on the way, she noticed that Topsy was following her. Lucy hurried back, opened the gate, and called to Topsy, "Come back in the yard. You have to stay home. I'm going to school."

But Topsy had been kept in her own yard so long that she wanted a change. She wagged her tail in reply, and stood just far enough away so that Lucy couldn't catch her. "Topsy, it's dangerous for you. You've got to stay home," Lucy commanded.

Topsy dodged and jumped and circled and refused to obey. Finally, Lucy tricked her. "Topsy, play dead," she ordered. Topsy lay down flat, rolled over on her back, and lay still.

Lucy made a quick grab, picked her up, and ran back to the house with her. Mother, who seemed to be feeling less well, had gone back upstairs to bed. Lucy called upstairs. "Watch Topsy like a hawk, Mother. She's trying to get out of the yard." And not waiting for Mother's faint answer, Lucy rushed off, already late for school.

Edward had refused to wait, so Gwin and Guinevere had taken him to the primary room, but Gwen was waiting at the parsonage gate. Together she and Lucy ran the half block to the school, through the door, and up the wooden stairs to their room.

Everyone else was in his place, so Lucy paused at the teacher's desk to excuse herself and Gwen. "I'm sorry, Miss Fothergill, but I had to take my dog home."

Miss Fothergill's frown changed to a smile. "So you've got a dog. What kind?" she asked, in a sugary drawl.

"Mostly fox terrier with a little bit of Boston bulldog."

"Oh, I love bulldogs, don't you?" Miss Fothergill's favorite topic was obviously dogs. Lucy stored this fact in her mind. You never knew when it might come in handy.

The morning classes began with seventh-grade American history. "I thought it would be awfully exciting if we all began with Columbus, way back at the beginning. Don't you think that would be a lot of fun?" Miss Fothergill beamed at them.

Nobody answered her, but if she had listened she might have heard a slight groan from the seventh grade and even a slight snicker from the eighth grade, where no one was supposed to be listening. Every year since the third grade, they had begun with Christopher Columbus and usually got no further than the opening of the Civil War. Then the next year, a new teacher started them again with Christopher Columbus.

This time Harvey Fischer, Jerry's brother, put up his hand. "Miss Fothergill, do you think we might do something on the election coming in November—and Columbus, too, of course," he suggested.

"An election isn't history yet, is it?" Miss Fothergill said, smiling at him. "Where I come from, down in Oklahoma, we don't discuss elections in school."

"But maybe we could study about the war and this election, maybe," Tony Alper said, and as he saw her face, he added, "that is, if we get in Columbus, too."

"Well, we'll start with Columbus, and perhaps later the election—" Miss Fothergill thought a moment. "No, children, it's not a good idea to study elections. You'll take sides, and there'll be arguments, and—no, really, we'll not say anything about the election until Wednesday morning, the day after the election. Then we'll just announce the results."

"There's going to be a big rally the night before the election—at Fischer's Hall," Julie Meizner said. "Everybody in the whole township will go to that."

"Then that's where you'll learn how presidents are elected," Miss Fothergill said with finality. "And now, wouldn't you all like to learn the names of Columbus' three ships and who gave him the money to come and all those interesting facts?"

The whole seventh grade wanted to yell, "No! We've already had Columbus!" But they could see that it was useless.

"And I want to explain about your reading class," Miss Fothergill went on. "This year we'll concentrate on poetry. I adore poetry, don't you?"

Dead silence. But Miss Fothergill obviously lived in a world of her own, and silence didn't faze her.

In the middle of the morning, a third-grader, Trudy Meizner, came in with a note for Miss Fothergill. She read it, looked up, and asked for a volunteer to go down to the primary room to help Miss Baxter. Lucy's hand was up first, so Miss Fothergill nodded, and Lucy ran downstairs with Trudy. Even before they opened the door to Miss Baxter's room, Lucy heard the rumpus.

Once inside, Lucy wished she hadn't been so quick to volunteer. This year the primary room was jam-packed with small children, three grades of them. And lots of them were first-graders.

There were exactly enough new little red chairs for each first-grader, yet one was somehow missing. As Lucy came in, Freddie Gratz pushed roly-poly Mamie Dolan off her chair so he could sit down. Then Mamie crowded in with Polly O'Neil, and that left so little room for Polly that she fell on the floor.

But up at the front of the room one little girl had taken two chairs—one for herself and one to hold her sweater. Very gently Miss Baxter was explaining, "Doris Flint, it's your first day at school, so you may not know that each child has only one chair."

Dorrie paid no attention, just went on smoothing her dress.

"Doris," Miss Baxter said a little more firmly, "you have to let Polly O'Neil have that chair and hang up your sweater in the hall."

Dorrie gave one look at Miss Baxter, opened her mouth, and began to howl. Miss Baxter looked terrified, as she moved toward the screaming Dorrie. And

Dorrie was watching at the same time she was having her tantrum. When Miss Baxter reached for her, Dorrie threw herself to the floor, hung onto both chairs, and opened her mouth even wider. "Yeoow!" Dorrie yowled. "They're my chairs! Mine!"

"No! Only one!" shouted Miss Baxter. The rest of the children were now absolutely quiet, each sitting like a small statue, except for Polly, who had no chair to sit on, and Davy Lowenstein, who was sobbing, "Mama, Mama!"

"Morrie and me'll tell our mama!" Dorrie raged on, now banging her heels as well as the chairs on the floor.

Miss Baxter looked helpless. Morrie stared out the window as though he'd never heard of a girl named Dorrie Flint. So Lucy went up to Dorrie, caught her by the flailing shoes, and yelled, "You stop it, Dorrie Flint!"

But Dorrie succeeded in kicking her feet free and then kicking Lucy in the shins. Miss Baxter retreated to her desk, and Lucy followed her. "Have you got any food we could put in Dorrie's mouth?" Lucy asked, putting her face close to Miss Baxter's in order to be heard. "Got anything sweet?"

Miss Baxter opened a desk drawer, brought out a cardboard box of lunch, and produced a piece of gooey banana cake with sticky white frosting between the layers. Lucy picked it up, then picked up Dorrie, who had begun to ease her howls as soon as she'd seen the cake. "Looks messy!" Dorrie made a face.

"You sit up in your chair, and you eat it!" Lucy ordered. So that's just what Dorrie did.

"Polly, that chair's for you now," Miss Baxter said. Polly edged up to Dorrie, swiftly snatched the extra chair, and carried it as far away as possible, all the time keeping her eye on Dorrie.

What Miss Baxter did next, Lucy thought, proved she might become a good teacher, even if she couldn't manage Dorrie. From another desk drawer she took out a large box of lollipops, as she explained, "I had these for a party I thought we might have someday. But I don't want one little girl to get a treat for bad behavior and the rest of you get nothing. And Morrie, how about helping Lucy and me to pass them out?"

By now Dorrie was a shambles of cake, sliced bananas, and frosting, but she rammed the last of it into her mouth to reach for a lollipop. Lucy watched Miss Baxter.

"Here's a lollipop for you too, Dorrie, since you now belong to the class, don't you? You've already learned that everyone has to share—nobody's special." And Miss Baxter held out to her a grape-flavored purple lollipop.

But Dorrie did not take it. She put her hands behind her back and loudly announced, "I specially hate grape! And I specially want cherry!"

"You'll get grape or none at all." Miss Baxter pronounced each word slowly and very distinctly, fixing her eyes on Dorrie, who stuck the purple lollipop in her pouting mouth without saying thank-you.

When noontime came, Miss Baxter thanked Lucy and told her that Mr. Grady had said some girl might come each day to help her. "Could you come regularly, do you think?" she asked. "The eighth-graders and the high-schoolers have to work on passing the state exams, you know, but couldn't you come?"

Lucy agreed, though as she looked around the room and saw not only Dorrie, Edward, and spoiled Davy

Lowenstein, but all three Kanes as well, she wondered whether Miss Fothergill's room might not be better. At least it was quieter.

At dinner Amory told of the projects his room would do. "We're each going to study a different tribe of Indians, and I've already looked up stuff on the Mandans, and I found they had ideas about the northern lights, and I bet you wish you knew," he teased, as he put a half-slice of bread in his gravy and rubbed it around his plate. "Glad I'm not under your roaring boring spell," he crowed.

"Tell me what you know—please, Amory," Lucy begged.

"Well, the Mandans believe that—" and he stopped to cram his mouth with bread and gravy. But Amory could eat and talk at once, so he continued, "They believe that northern lights are the flames under the pots they boil their enemies and prisoners in."

"How awful!" Lucy shouted. "That can't be true!"

"It's right in the book. And now everytime you look at your old lights, you can think your spell probably means you'll get boiled and—"

"Cut it out, Amory," Father said. "That's enough horror for one course. What do we have for dessert, Caroline?"

Mother laughed. "I really didn't plan the dessert to go with the dinner conversation, but we're having boiled pudding."

"With lots of hard sauce?" Amory asked. "Maybe the Mandans serve hard sauce with their—"

"That's enough!" Father bellowed. "Amory, you clear the plates and help your mother bring in the pudding."

Topsy
Is
Sent Away

~~~

As they sat eating the pudding, Father asked to see the snapshots that had been returned to Lucy in the mail the day before. From the envelope, along with the negatives and the small photos, dropped a printed slip. It advertised a competition the Kodak company was having for prize snapshots. Glancing at the notice, Lucy saw there was one prize for pictures taken by people under twelve years of age.

"Look, Mother, couldn't I try for a prize?"

"Is it for cash?" Amory asked. "Or only some dumb certificate of award?"

"Not cash," Lucy answered, "but they make a big enlargement of a prize-winning picture." She spread her prints around her place at the table. "Which should I send? Three is all they allow. What do you choose, Father?"

Father picked out three and passed them to Mother for her approval. "Yes," Mother said, as she passed them back to Lucy, "these are the clearest and each one is different."

Lucy gave a long look at all her snaps, and she could see the flat field in front of the house wasn't much, and her snaps of people were blurred by one wiggler always, and even the remains of the elevator fire made a dull picture. But the far-off Pembina River in its wide valley, the threshing rig, and their own house were all clear and complete.

"Our house—won't judges of a competition think it's an awfully ordinary house?" she asked Mother, who replied at once.

"I love it, except that I wish it had twice as many closets and a couple more rooms and a bathroom—" Mother was wound up.

Father interrupted. "Get those snaps ready to mail at once, Lucy, or your mother will have it rebuilt into a palace!"

"Oh, dear, they don't notify the winners until Christmas," Lucy said, "and it's all decided in the East, in New York State."

"Who said you'd win?" Amory teased. "You've got the chance of a—" He didn't finish what Lucy knew was not a compliment.

"Lucy, don't forget I told Sarah Lowenstein that you'd take Davy home after school this afternoon, while she comes for her lesson," Mother reminded Lucy when she was leaving for school.

"Mother! That Davy is in the first grade now, and he doesn't need to be taken home," Lucy objected.

"I promised," Mother said. "Besides, Davy is their only boy, and you remember your father's telling you how important a boy is in a Jewish family that follows its religion so strictly."

"Sometimes I wonder where girls come in," Lucy said bitterly. "You say Edward is so important because the Owens are British, and Father says the farmers are happiest when they get boys, and now there's Davy. Aren't there any families that want girls?"

"You can't imagine how excited we were to get you, so excited that we forgot to ask about that spell." Mother laughed.

"Funny we don't hear from Miss Ross, isn't it?" Lucy asked, standing dreamily at the open door.

"We'll have to write again soon if—but gracious me, there you stand in a wide-open door as though it were July instead of a sharp fall day!"

So Lucy explained to Miss Fothergill about leaving early to take Davy, and at 3:30 she met him in the primary room and rushed him home to his waiting mother in the store. Lucy wanted to get back before her room was let out, but Mrs. Butler spied her and called, "Lucy, come see Noreen."

Mrs. Butler was pushing a squeaky old baby carriage, but she looked like a happy mother, out parading a first baby. "Nora's gone out to Mrs. Towne's to help until we all go to Canada—just before Christmas we're going, soon as my old man gets the money —and look at Noreen. Isn't she pretty? Prettiest Butler baby we've ever had!" Mrs. Butler paused.

Lucy looked down into the carriage, and there was no doubt about it. Noreen was already pretty, and she was only a month old. "She is pretty, she is!" Lucy sounded amazed, for all the Butlers, even Nora, were a homely family with squinty eyes, and here was a beautiful Butler.

Then Lucy excused herself and ran for the school. Her room was empty, or empty except for Miss Fothergill, who filled most of the front of it. Lucy looked in to say goodnight, but Miss Fothergill called her.

"You've got a dog. I'm wondering what your family is doing about distemper." Without waiting for Lucy's reply, she went on. "My Mr. Guggums—that's my dog's name, did you know?"

"The whole town knows that," Lucy said to herself, but to Miss Fothergill she only nodded.

"I'm so afraid for him. He'd never survive—poor old boy, he's very frail." Miss Fothergill spoke fearfully.

Lucy wondered for a moment whether they were speaking of the same dog. Very frail? That whopping, big old dog?

"If I'd only known about the distemper here, I'd have left him with somebody else, though I'd have missed my Mr. Guggums awfully. Dogs are like people to me. Aren't they to you?" Miss Fothergill smiled at Lucy as friend to friend.

"I don't think you need to worry about Mr.—" Lucy couldn't bring herself to say that ridiculous name, so she began again. "My father says that the germs are around all the time, but it's the very young dogs that die. He says older dogs have probably had mild cases and are immune."

"That's the best news I've heard since I came to Wales. When I go home after the teachers' meeting, I can feed my Mr. Guggums and not think it may be his last meal. I've been so afraid!" She still looked afraid when she said it. "Thank you, Lucy, and now please take this note down to Mrs. O'Neil's room as you go out. These stairs will be the death of me."

As Lucy came to Mrs. O'Neil's room, Hilda Dickerman was coming out with Mrs. O'Neil beside her. "Don't you worry, Hilda, it's your first year in a town school, but you'll soon catch on. In no time, you'll be up to everyone," Mrs. O'Neil said comfortingly, and Hilda did look happy as she left.

Taking the note from Lucy, Mrs. O'Neil invited her into the vacant room. "Miss Baxter tells me what a help you were to her this morning. Now I'd like a little help, too," she began.

Lucy's first thought was that she might have to help in those grades also, and she remembered there were three Scheler boys and two Butlers in that room. But before she could concoct an excuse, Mrs. O'Neil explained.

"When I was getting acquainted with Hilda—you must know her?—she told me that last year one of her brothers died of infantile. I've brought my Polly here, and now I find there's infantile and everybody says not to worry, but—tell me, does your family worry about it?" The smiling, cheerful Mrs. O'Neil suddenly looked panic-stricken.

"Of course they're afraid, especially my mother. But hasn't anyone told you that infantile is mostly done when we have a heavy frost, like that one a couple of nights ago?" Lucy searched Mrs. O'Neil's face, and she saw that a widow with one child needed more assurance than a seventh-grader could give her.

"My father's always at the bank, and he'd be glad to tell you not to worry, and come someday soon to see my mother. Bring Polly, too," Lucy invited.

On the way home, Lucy thought of the three

women teachers—Miss Baxter who was afraid in her first job, Miss Fothergill so fearful about her doddering old dog, and now Mrs. O'Neil in a panic over infantile. "They're all afraid of something," Lucy said to herself, "but I suppose their fears are what people call sensible ones and not like mine." Yet her fear about Mother, wasn't that sensible? She wished she could just ask Mother. But somehow she couldn't.

Then behind her she heard a dog running on the wooden sidewalk. Turning around, Lucy saw it was Topsy. "Topsy! You runaway!" she screamed. Topsy, delighted to see her, came bounding up. "Whatever can I do to keep you safe from germs?" Lucy scolded, as she picked up the little terrier and carried her home.

When Sarah's lesson was done, Lucy asked Mother, "How did Topsy get out again?" Mother explained that Sarah had let her out by mistake as she'd come in. "Can't you possibly watch her, Mother, just while I'm in school?"

"I try, Lucy, but I'm just not up to chasing Topsy these days," Mother apologized. And Lucy noticed how wearily she spoke.

When later Lucy recounted the fears of the three teachers, Mother said, "Miss Baxter will get over being afraid of her children. And Miss Fothergill's old dog won't live forever, but he won't die of distemper. Mrs. O'Neil's fear is the one I share." Mother shook her head. "Against infantile, we're so helpless."

"Nobody told me, Mother, until today at school, that Mrs. Smith took Roger to the hospital in Grand Forks, and he'll always be in a wheelchair, and can't ever walk again." Lucy looked sharply at Mother. "Did you know it and not tell me?"

"No, I didn't hear about it, either, until today, from Sarah. Sarah says Mrs. Smith is taking him back to Milwaukee, where she came from, as soon as he can be moved. And Mort Smith's selling the farm and everything on it. Then he'll go, too."

"And Roger won't ever be back?" Lucy tried not to believe it.

"Not likely, poor boy," Mother said sadly.

Lucy knew better than to complain again about Topsy's running loose, with so many worse problems around. But obviously Topsy was leading a risky life. This she knew, too.

She was not prepared, however, for the suggestion Father made a few days later. She suspected there was a reason for his driving her to school on Friday noon, and when he kept the Regal in low speed so they could talk, she knew something was wrong.

"I've been looking for a hired girl to help your mother, but there isn't one in the whole blamed county at this season," he began. Now Lucy was really alarmed. Hiring a girl meant a family crisis.

The family hired girls only when there was a serious illness. Hired girls, of course, lived at the house and became part of the family. Unlike the maid at Grandfather's, a hired girl ate with them. And either she did all the talking, or else she was what Mother called "the quiet kind," so quiet that Mother spent the whole meal trying to get her to say something—anything at all.

After the last girl had left, Mother had said, "Never again, Harry." And Lucy clearly remembered that Father had joked, "Only if someone's dying! Nothing short of that."

"Is Mother dreadfully sick?" Lucy asked. "I'll do

anything," she promised. "Should I stay home from school some of the time and be hired girl until you can find one?" Lucy meant it as an honest offer, but she was aware that she'd be a total loss as a hired girl. The hired girls who'd helped them before were always nearly as tall as Father, and their arms were the arms of what Father called "good, hard workers," with wide elbows, round, red forearms, and hands so big that they could hold two sauce dishes in each one. Beside them Lucy felt like a dwarf, and not a very useful dwarf either.

Father looked amused. "I like your offering to do it," he said, "but things aren't quite that bad. Besides Amory and I can't live on cornmeal mush, and that's still your specialty, isn't it?"

By now they were beside the school. "But what I do have to ask will be hard for you, Lucy. For the long winter ahead, your mother and I think it would ease things a little if Topsy were at a farm—until spring."

"Send Topsy away? Out to a farm? For all winter?" Lucy couldn't believe her ears.

"It's not forever." Father spoke very soberly. "When the weather is good and your mother feels better, we'll bring your Topsy home. Could you try it? For Mother's sake?" he asked.

"But Topsy's my baby and my best friend, too," Lucy argued. "I'm with her even more than with Gwen, and I brought her up."

"Won't you try it? Too much is too much for your mother these days, and Topsy is one thing too much," Father went on explaining. "Mort Smith's moving away you know, but Topsy's family of dogs will be at the Klebers' farm—over beyond Sarles. I thought that might be a good place."

He bent down and saw she was about to cry. "Mr. Kleber's in town today, and I thought it might be easier for you if you didn't have too long to say good-bye. Should I just have him take her before you come home from school this afternoon?"

"No, no—you drive me out with her to Klebers' on Sunday. I want to see where she'll sleep and what her brothers are like now and who'll feed her and who'll pet her." Lucy's tears were now in full stream, and Father handed her his big handkerchief. "Please wait till Sunday," she begged between sobs. "Then I promise I'll be brave and wait for her until spring." And she held up the handkerchief to cover her whole face, since the children were all coming in from the back playground and going into the school.

"All right. If the weather is fit, I'll drive you and Topsy out on Sunday. It's a long way and the roads are bad, but I'll tell Mr. Kleber we'll come then." Father tried to mop her tears with the other half of the large handkerchief.

The last bell was ringing, and she had to go into her schoolroom. Snuffles from a cold no one noticed, but snuffles from crying would make everyone stare, and staring she didn't want. So she caught her lower lip between her teeth, winked very hard, and rubbed her coat sleeve across her face. Then she got out of the auto, went to the school door, and turned to wave as Father drove off to Main Street. Slowly she entered and climbed to the seventh-grade room, where Miss Fothergill was calling the roll.

When Lucy came home from school, Topsy jumped around her as happily as ever. "You don't know, Topsy, what's ahead of you," Lucy said gloomily. Topsy stood on her hind legs and twirled three waltz steps as her only reply.

But Mother called from the living room, "Lucy dear, I'm sad for you, but your father and I can't think of any other way. Besides, distemper is worse in Wales this year than anywhere else. Mr. Kleber told us there's not a single case around them."

Lucy had forgotten distemper, and this was the one comfort she had. A winter on a farm might save Topsy's life. Yet she thought of it as a long, dismal time ahead, and she spent every minute of the next day with Topsy. She even used a whole roll of film for snapshots of Topsy—in her costume, out of her costume, sitting up to beg, and lying down to play dead.

On Sunday Amory decided to stay home and play games with Stan. Mother, as usual, was lying on the sofa. So Lucy and Father, with Topsy snuggled into the lap robe, made the trip alone.

When they got to the Klebers', after driving most of the morning, Lucy saw that Topsy's brothers had grown much larger than Topsy, but they seemed not to want to eat her. In no time Topsy was racing with them around the farmyard as happily as she'd raced to and from the back gate with Lucy. There were no Kleber children, so no one would tease her or be mean. And the warm place near the calves in the barn, where the dogs slept, looked cozy, as well as the corner of the kitchen, where Mrs. Kleber said Topsy could sleep when the barn was freezing cold.

Since it was a long, cold drive home, they stopped for only a plate of hot mince pie before Lucy gave Topsy a last squeezing hug, and she and Father climbed back in the Regal. All the way home Father

told stories and jokes and talked of what she'd be doing in the weeks until Christmas.

But Lucy was not a good audience. Her lap missed
Topsy; her arms needed Topsy. But she knew she
mustn't say anything to upset Mother. So when, late
in the afternoon, they came in the kitchen door and
Mother asked, "How did it go?" it was Father who
answered, "Fine. It'll be a good winter home for
Topsy, won't it, Lucy?"

Lucy, who had no words and no voice to say anything, nodded and ran in by the living-room stove to
get warm. Later, she couldn't swallow a bite of supper, so Mother and Father just looked wisely at each
other and let her go to bed with only a drink of hot
cocoa and a cookie. Both of them gave her an extra
tight goodnight hug; and Father, though he was tired
from the long, bumpy drive, came upstairs and read
aloud twice as many chapters as usual from *David
Copperfield.*

Second
Sight at
an Auction

~·~

On Monday morning the only person who truly understood how much Lucy missed Topsy was Gwin. In most ways Lucy and Gwin were too different to be close friends, but Topsy they both loved. "And you won't see her again until spring?" Gwin asked in a shocked tone. "I'd hate my mama and papa if they did that to me!"

"Well, you've seen—my mother's lying down so much nowadays that Topsy might have run away and caught distemper and died." Lucy wanted it to sound good, but to herself she also wondered how the folks could have sent Topsy away.

School took her mind off Topsy, especially the hour or more a day she spent helping Miss Baxter. She had no time to think while Johnnie Kane was putting his foot in the aisle to trip someone and Edward was collecting all the new crayons for himself and Mamie Dolan was crying because the boys called her Fatty and Dorrie was pinching anyone who came near her. Miss Baxter was coping better, as Lucy told Mother, but she still was afraid of some of the children. You could see it in her eyes.

The Stone Age Girls kept score on how often Mr. Grady went downstairs to see Miss Baxter, but Lucy reminded them he went just as often to Mrs. O'Neil's room.

"But she's an old widow with a girl in the first grade," Guinevere said.

"So he's going to marry Miss Baxter," Gwin said very definitely.

"It couldn't be Miss Fothergill. She's already married to Mr. Guggums." Gwen giggled. "She doesn't love anything the way she loves that dog. Not really human, is she?"

Lucy laughed with the girls, but thinking of Topsy, she asked herself, "Maybe I'm not really human either?" Coming home each day with no Topsy to wiggle a welcome was hard. And each week it grew harder. Yet she knew it was best. At least she tried to tell herself it was. It would be worse if something happened to Mother.

But it grew harder and harder during the next weeks for Lucy to eat. Whether it was the lump in her throat or the effort to keep from saying anything that might upset Mother or just that she had no appetite—no matter what it was, she simply couldn't swallow her food. Mother made her favorite cookies, planned tea parties for after school with the girls, and had milk and chocolate cupcakes for her all the time.

But it was Amory who polished off all the extra-fancy cooking, and Lucy couldn't eat more than a few spoonfuls. Even when Father brought home some ice cream from the new drugstore, she couldn't eat. Since both Father and Lucy were mad about ice cream, Mother stared at Lucy in a troubled way. And the very next day Father drove both Mother and Lucy to the butcher shop to be weighed on the only scales in the village.

Ed the butcher was in high spirits, but his joking was no comfort to Mother. "Step on the scales, Lucy," he said as he began putting one small iron disk after another on the hooked bar. "Why, you're shrinking—just like salt pork that's cooked in too hot a pan, and *poof*—it disappears."

Mother glanced at the reading on the scales but said nothing about Lucy's similarity to salt pork. Then she stepped on the scales herself. Before she could place heavier disks on the hook, the butcher was weighing her, too.

"Mrs. Johnston, I hate to tell you, but you've put on even more pounds than Lucy has lost." He shook his head. "How do you account for that?" he asked.

Without answering, Mother ordered some beef ground for meat loaf. Later Mother laughed about Lucy as salt pork, but the next noon, Lucy overheard Mother talking seriously with Father.

"I'm worried about Lucy. No child should lose weight that way. Dr. Carmer's taken a patient to Grand Forks, but you go to Langdon tomorrow—why not take Lucy to Dr. Stewart?"

So it wasn't a surprise to Lucy at suppertime when Mother said, "You've not had your regular checkup this year, so tomorrow you'll skip school, and your father will take you with him to Langdon to see Dr. Stewart."

"Let's make it a real junket," Father said. "On the way home we'll stop at Mort Smith's farm for his auction sale."

Lucy wasn't fooled. This wasn't for a regular checkup. The folks wanted to find out why she didn't eat, and she didn't eat because all the time her stomach felt sad. "Can my missing Topsy make my stomach sad?" she asked herself. She'd heard of heartaches and broken hearts from sadness—but a sad stomach? No one would believe that, so she said nothing.

Amory, who came rushing in for supper, was so lively that by contrast Lucy saw she must seem droopy. He hurried to the table, talking nonstop about the Cave Men's plans for Halloween. Then he suddenly looked at Lucy, paused, and said, "Gee whiz, Lucy's awful white. She sick or something?"

That from Amory, who lived his own life and never noticed how anyone looked, was a shocker. "What makes her so white anyway? She's as white as those white rats Mr. Donner had in his lab cage last year when we—"

"Omit the white rats," Father cut in abruptly. "Lucy needs some tonic, we think, perhaps some cod-liver oil, but she's your sister and not a white rat." Mother said nothing.

Right after dinner the following day, Lucy and Father set off for Langdon. It was the end of October, and winter was not far off. As Lucy waved goodbye to Mother, who was watching from the living-room window, she saw how snugly the house was prepared for the long, bitter cold. Storm windows and storm doors were on, dirt and straw were banked around the foundation; and she knew the cellar was filled with potatoes, carrots, and turnips, and with cabbages hanging from the beams above.

Father must have been thinking somewhat the same thing, because he said, "The snow we've had so far has melted, but soon we'll get the real thing. Time I put this auto up on jacks in the barn—this may be the last time I'll have it on the road until spring."

The late-October air was cold, and the upright windshield held off the wind only long enough for it to come roaring around the sides of the metal-framed glass and against their faces. The first nine miles south of Wales were the usual rutted dirt road, and now that the harvest was done, the stubble fields and the bleak plowed land were not much to look at. The birds had all flown south, the gophers were underground, and even the farms they passed looked deserted.

When they turned for the eleven miles east to Langdon, the road was better, as if to remind people that Langdon was the county seat. When they drew near, Father became talkative. "Your Johnston cousins are in school, so we won't try to see them. I have a brief errand at the courthouse, and then we'll go to Dr. Stewart."

At the red-brick courthouse, Lucy went in to get warm. She sat on a long, hard bench in the corridor, and while Father looked up some records, she thought of Luke Morgan, the man who had been kept in the jail at the back of the building and whom she'd helped to go back to Canada. Now he was in the war, and war made her think of Miss Ross and the letter that was never answered. "Probably sunk by a submarine," she said to herself, liking the sound but not the idea.

Soon they were back in the Regal and driving the three blocks to the doctor's house. There in the outer office, Lucy was left with a red-haired woman in a nurse's uniform while Father went in to talk with Dr. Stewart.

"I'm Mrs. Stewart—I was Meg Ross before I married—and Dr. Stewart tells me you wrote my cousin Janet about a spell," the red-haired woman said. "We haven't heard from her for weeks and weeks—mail gone down, we suppose." For a moment she looked over Lucy's head and out the window, as though she were thinking of some far-off place.

"Janet always had a lot of lore in her head, like being born under the spell of the northern lights. But some things she did know about—that's sure." Mrs. Stewart seemed able to talk without Lucy's asking questions, so Lucy sat still and quiet.

"Now the only thing I ever heard about the northern lights putting a spell on folks was that they could give a person second sight."

Second sight! Lucy was fascinated, but Mrs. Stewart said no more. Father came out of the inner office and motioned for Lucy to go in alone. Dr. Stewart was all business. His *Hello, Lucy* was almost abrupt. Then he checked her heart, her ears, and her breath in and out of her lungs and he banged her knees with a little hammer.

Finally he leaned back in his swivel chair and gave her a long, searching look. "Lucy, what's the matter?" He cocked his head at her and asked wisely, "Are you worried about your mother?"

"Yes, she seems so different," Lucy said. "But she says she'll be good as new in the spring. That's why in the spring I can get back my Topsy." Somehow just saying the word *Topsy* to someone who didn't know Topsy brought out the whole story. "She's my dog and my best friend, and we had to put her on a farm until spring," and here the tears began to roll down Lucy's cheeks. "I miss her so much that my stomach is sad all the time."

"So that's it," said Dr. Stewart, as he took out a piece of gauze for her to wipe her eyes. "I was afraid it was that spell you told me about." He patted her on the head, left her in the office chair, and went out to speak to Father.

"You can cure her better than I, Mr. Johnston," he said. His voice was warm and comforting now. "I've heard of people feeling sick as a dog, but this is the first time I've had a patient sick *for* a dog." Lucy didn't hear what came next, for she was busy blowing her nose and getting her tears under control.

Quickly she was back in her winter clothes, said good-bye to both the Stewarts, and then Father was tucking the heavy robe tightly around her in the front seat. For a mile or two Father said nothing. When he did speak he wasn't scolding, only remarking.

"Sometimes I don't think you're as bright as those school tests say you are, Lucy. I'll never understand why you didn't tell us how much Topsy meant to you."

"I thought everybody knew—and you did say not to upset Mother, didn't you?" Lucy spoke in her I'll-have-the-last-word voice. Father didn't reply. He took his hand off the wheel a moment and thumped her on her blanketed lap, not a hard thump, simply a way of saying, "Everything will be all right now."

Shortly after they turned the corner to drive the last nine miles to Wales, Father pointed out the Mort

Smiths' farmyard. "We'll stop there, but not for long," he explained. "I should see Mort, and Mr. Kinser is the auctioneer today."

"Could I bid for something, Father? You know Topsy was born here, and I'd love to have some little thing—maybe for Topsy, maybe for me." But it was Roger she really thought of.

"We have to buy something—that's sure. So if I give you five dimes, you might even get two small things," Father said.

As they stopped at the edge of the crowded farmyard, Lucy heard Mr. Kinser's selling spiel loud and clear, over the din of people calling and children running around screaming and cows bawling and dogs barking. He was holding up a big framed mirror and shouting, "How much for this clear and uncracked mirror? Brings you seven years of good luck, and look at the mahogany frame, all hand-carved mahogany—"

" 'Taint mahogany—only pine!" yelled a woman.

"Very best grade of pine," Mr. Kinser drowned out the woman's voice with his bellow. "How much am I bid?" Someone called out "Five dollars," and Mr. Kinser echoed the shout. "Five dollars, a man says. Who'll take it up to six? Six dollars! Six dollars! There, Mrs. Dolan bids six! Now who'll bid seven for seven years of good luck. Who'll bid seven?"

Lucy felt that dollar-bidding was out of her range, so she began looking around her. The men were gathered by the barn, and the women around the back porch, where Mr. Kinser stood, surrounded by iron kettles and pieces of carpet, kitchen chairs and cartons of tinware, a cream separator, and bedsprings, headboards, and mattresses. On a chair lay a pair of skates, useless for Roger now.

Father went toward the barn, and Lucy stood uncertainly, shy among so many strangers. As she waited for Mr. Kinser to hold up something her five dimes might buy, Mrs. Towne waved to her and came over.

"Plan to buy something, Lucy?" she asked.

"I've got only five dimes, Mrs. Towne."

"What I'd do, Lucy, is bid on one of those shoe boxes," Mrs. Towne said cheerfully. "Any box like that is what you call a *pig in a poke*—you never know what's in it until you open it after you've bought it. Sometimes it's a real bargain."

Mrs. Towne made it seem so attractive that Lucy went closer, fixed her eye on a tan shoe box, and while she waited for it to be auctioned, she told herself, "If my spell gives me second sight, I can see inside a box. That one holds what I want—a treasure."

Soon Mr. Kinser held up the tan box, yelling, "Who'll take a chance on this?" He hefted it up and down in his hand. "So heavy it might have a gold brick in it. Who'll buy a gold brick?" Then he shook it near his ear. "It rattles, so it may be pure gold nuggets, or several small gold bricks. Now who's interested in pure gold? What am I bid on this pig-in-a-poke shoe box of gold?"

Lucy shouted, "Twenty cents!"

Mr. Kinser recognized her. "There's a little girl lives in my block in Wales, and she knows a good thing when she sees it—"

"But she doesn't see it! Take the cover off so she can see," a big girl yelled.

Mr. Kinser kept on calling. "Who'll bid thirty cents for this box? Nobody want to buy gold today? But mind, I'm not guaranteeing it's packed with gold—but it does weigh a—Lena Drake, you bid thirty cents? Thirty, thirty— Who'll up it to forty? Forty? Going at thirty, going, going—"

"Forty cents!" Lucy shrieked in a voice she hardly recognized as her own.

"Going, going, gone at forty cents!" Mr. Kinser brought the sale swiftly to a close, and Lucy went forward to take the shoe box from him. While he shifted his pitch to the merits of a boy's wagon, with four strong wheels, Lucy scurried to the auto to open her box. Here was the first test of her second sight.

She couldn't untie the knot in the string, so she

slipped the cord off one corner, loosened it entirely, and lifted the flat top. The entire box was jammed with picture postcards—old cards, bent, faded, and worn; pictures of buildings, mountains, parks, and city streets. And she had paid forty cents for that!

When she turned over some of the cards, she saw that the names of places were in foreign languages, and the stamps were foreign stamps. Perhaps in geography class they'd be useful, or she could give them to Amory for Christmas, but they were not her idea of a treasure. "So much for my second sight from the northern lights," she said bitterly to herself.

With only one dime left, she sat and waited for Father. When he climbed in, she showed him her stack of old postcards, and before she thought, she blamed her poor bargain on Mrs. Stewart's talk of second sight. "That is what second sight means, isn't it?" Lucy asked. "Only mine doesn't work."

Father laughed. "Well, I wouldn't depend much on second sight at an auction. And what will your Mother say about a doctor who prescribes a dog-cure for you, and his wife who says you might have second sight?"

Then he answered her question. "Second sight does mean seeing what others can't see, but usually it's seeing into the future, or sometimes the past. Let's not have you thinking you're some kind of prophet, Lucy. Outgrowing your fears because a spell is done is one thing, but second sight—forget it!" But Lucy didn't forget.

The Cave Men
Become
Boy Scouts

Back home, Lucy opened the driveway gate and the wide barn door for Father to put away the Regal, but then instead of running to the house, she climbed the wall ladder to the loft.

"What in the mischief are you doing?" Father asked.

"Stay there a moment," Lucy answered. "I'll hand down Topsy's basket bed to you. I'm going to dust it and put it behind the range for when we bring Topsy home."

Later as she lugged the bed through the shed, she heard Father talking. "And I've always thought I knew so much about children. How could I have been so blind?"

Lucy paused to hear Mother's answer. "It's always

our own children that we don't understand, Harry."
And as Lucy came into the kitchen, Mother went on,
"So on Sunday your father is driving you way out to
Klebers' again to bring Topsy home. I do hope it
doesn't snow before then."

In the living room Amory was reading, with his
feet propped up on the warm nickel rim around the
stove. "You going to bring back that mutt?" he asked,
not crossly, only to say something.

Mother surprised Lucy by replying, "Indeed, and
we'll be glad to have the dog back and Lucy well
again. Now on Sunday, Amory, you'll have to represent the family at Sunday school—it's such a small
school this year that—"

"Me go for all of us?" Amory broke in. "But I—"

Before he could go any further, Father said severely, "You'll go." Then he chuckled. "You'll go,
and no stealing coins out of the collection, either."

"Harry, don't talk that way," Mother protested.
"Just because he borrowed Lucy's gold coin."

"Borrowed! He picked the lock on my box!" At
once she thought of her box of cards that Father had
brought in. "Look, Mother, do you think these are
worth anything?" Lucy dumped them on the table.

Mother picked up a few, turned them to look at the
stamps, and what she said next renewed Lucy's faith
in her second sight. "I'm not a stamp expert, but I
know Mrs. Smith had mail from a great-uncle who
traveled all over the world. These stamps might be
valuable."

"Good idea!" Father said. "And I know just the
person for you to ask, Lucy. Father Van Mert has a
stamp collection and a stack of stamp catalogs. Tomorrow's Saturday, so you take the boxful to him,

but he'll have to look them up. Don't expect instant appraisal—and don't expect a fortune. They're in bad condition, but he might want them to complete sets."

"How much did you pay?" Amory asked.

Now that the cards might be worth cash, Lucy was quick to reply, "Only forty cents."

"Where'd you get all the luck? Now you'll get rich, and I slaved in the Schneiders' fields and I'm broke and—"

"Oh, shut up, Amory!" Father barked; and when Lucy stared and Mother looked pained, Father didn't apologize, but he did change the subject. "This evening I'll make tick-tacks for you Stone Age Girls for Halloween. How about you Cave Men, Amory?"

"That's kid stuff. We've got other ideas," Amory sneered.

Father looked closely at him, but Mother said, "I've been saving empty spools for months, some very large ones, too."

Tick-tacks were Father's specialty. He knew exactly how to cut the notches in empty spools, fasten and wind the string around each one, and then with a little stick through the hole, the tick-tack was ready to pull along someone's window on Halloween. For such a small noisemaker, the big racketing clatter could startle anyone, especially in the dark.

When Lucy took her cards the next day to Father Van Mert, she used the front door to avoid Magic, who was often flying around the back porch. Mrs. Butler answered the knock.

"He'll be here in a moment. He's got no housekeeper yet, so I'm helping now and then, and I brought my Noreen, my baby, but she's asleep up-stairs and—"

Father Van Mert appeared, and Mrs. Butler went back to work; but Lucy had noticed that it was no longer Nora's baby to Mrs. Butler but "my baby." This was what Mother had predicted.

"So it's Lucy Johnston," Father Van Mert said. "What can I do for you?" He smiled at her just as he had that first August morning, only now he was a friend and not a stranger.

She explained her errand, showed him the cards, and he took the box from her with such a grin that she knew stamps must mean as much to him as model trains did to Mr. Owen. After a quick look he said, "I'll be glad to pay you two dollars. I've been search-ing for some of these. You're a very lucky girl," he told her, and she was sure of it.

On Sunday morning, Lucy and Father set off in the auto, with the top up and the side curtains on. This time it was not rain they had to keep out, but the sharp cold. There was frost in the air. Mother had insisted Lucy wear not only all her winter sweaters and her heavy coat, but her winter underwear as well. Ordinarily Lucy complained loudly about that long-legged underwear. But today she had pulled it on, yanked her long stockings over it, and never even grumbled.

Two flat tires on the road held them up, so it was midafternoon before they arrived at the farm. Father knocked at the back door, and when he called, "It's the Johnstons, Mrs. Kleber," Topsy recognized Fa-ther's deep voice. She began to bark and yip and almost shriek. The door opened, and before they could put foot inside, Topsy was out and jumping at Lucy's legs and hands and higher and higher, up to her face.

Far from having forgotten Lucy, Topsy had a fit of joy. She kept leaping, circling, and yipping until Father said, "For goodness' sake, Lucy, quiet that dog so I can explain to Mrs. Kleber."

So while Lucy hugged Topsy close against her chest, Father spoke with Mrs. Kleber. She insisted they have hot mince pie—"just like last time"—but they ate hastily, and in no time they were back in the auto for the long drive home.

"The dark will catch us on those last miles," Father said to Lucy, but she didn't care about anything. Her Topsy was snuggled on her lap once more.

When dusk had changed to dark and they were not far from home, they saw clearly against the black sky great blazing fires in all directions. Lucy knew what they were, so she wasn't frightened, and Father was delighted with the show.

Always on such a windless night, before the season of snow and after the fall rains were done, farmers all over the township set fire to their stacks of useless straw left by threshing rigs.

"Five, ten, fourteen." Lucy tried to count the globes of fire on the horizon, as more and more were lighted.

Then while she was still trying to number them, Father said, "Look! Look around, over there to the north. Your own lights, the northern lights again." And all the northern sky was lit with streaks and glowing streamers of light.

"It must be a celebration for me and Topsy this time, and I'm going to keep her with me always after this," Lucy declared.

With Topsy home again, Lucy went off to school Monday morning happier than she'd been in weeks. And though Miss Fothergill made her class repeat over and over again the lines from the poem about autumn, when the "trees in the apple orchard with fruit are bending down"—definitely a silly poem for October in North Dakota, where all the apples came in wooden boxes on the freight train—still Lucy loved every minute of the day.

At supper, both Father and Mother knew that Topsy was under the table and Lucy was feeding her the choicest bits of cold roast beef, but they only smiled across the table at each other and said nothing to Lucy.

"Halloween's tomorrow night, Amory," Father began. "Lucy's clubhouse has been filled with coal for the winter, and it's time for you Cave Men to close the cave."

"But I do close it all the time," Amory argued. "Nobody's fallen in for weeks."

"The cave season is over," Father replied. "I've been thinking that when you boys begin meeting indoors and not in a cave, you shouldn't be the Cave Men any longer. Why not reorganize as Boy Scouts? I'll meet with you once a week."

"Okay, what's the deal?" Amory asked.

"With only three of you, we can't have an official troop. Perhaps by spring some of the boys from nearby farms can come in, but for now—well, here's the *Scout Guide* that I bought," he said, handing Amory the thick book.

Amory at once began ruffling through the pages. "What's this about a Scout being polite? We won't make a specialty of that, will we?" Amory looked sharply at Father. "Are you trying to sell me something?"

"It wouldn't do you boys any harm," Mother said.

"But if the Cave Men become Boy Scouts, what about us Stone Age Girls?" Lucy asked.

"Bunch of savages! You're not good for anything," Amory said.

"I've thought of your club too, Lucy," Father began. "You know that your mother can't do as much for the Sunday school as usual, so you've all got to take more responsibility, a whole lot more in things like the Christmas pageant, for instance."

"Mercy, Harry, must you talk about Christmas when it's not yet November?" Mother wailed.

The next night Mother gave both Amory and Lucy old sheets to dress as ghosts. Lucy took her tick-tack, and Amory, when Mother wasn't watching, took a bar of Ivory soap to write on people's windows. He hurried to join the boys, and Lucy went toward the parsonage.

With the Owens, she raced all over town, rattling at windows and then rushing off into the dark. But even with the big sheet wrapped over her coat, she grew colder and colder.

"My second sight tells me I'm freezing to death," she told the girls. They had been excited about her story of second sight, but now they were shivering too much to discuss it, as they ran for their warm houses.

At noon the day after Halloween, Father came in, looking like a thundercloud. In a few minutes Amory breezed in from school. "What's for dinner?" he asked Mother.

Before she could answer, Father barked in a tremendous voice, "Amory, what's this I hear about your putting Mrs. Towne's buggy on top of the livery stable? And were you in the bunch that tried to put her horse up there, too?"

"Well, you see—" Amory always began his excuses very slowly. "I was there, but you never told me not to put a buggy up on a roof, and anyway I didn't do it alone."

"What kind of dummy do you think I am?" Father roared. "Of course you didn't do it alone! But somebody saw you standing on the roof, and the other boys pushing the buggy up some planks leaned against the side of the stable. And now there's a big hole in the roof, and George Henderson came in and handed me the bill for getting it fixed."

Father was getting redder and redder in the face. "And Mrs. Towne's horse—that poor animal's so skittish today that nobody could hitch her. And they tell me you were up on the roof trying to pull that horse up the planks, while the other boys stood below." Father glared at Amory until his eyes bugged out. "Why in tarnation do you have to be the only boy everybody recognizes?"

"I think—maybe it's because I'm such a good climber. I am good, you know. And I'm not so big as the other boys. And that's really why I was the only one on the roof." Amory smiled, but the smile soon faded, as Father went on.

"And Butlers' privy was tipped over last night—a family with ten children and you tip over their outhouse! How in the dickens do you think they're going to manage—" Father must have noticed that Mother was upset, so he shifted his rage a little. "Mr.

Butler says you were one of the trio of ghosts that turned it over. Were you, Amory?"

"Ghosts are awful hard to tell apart, aren't they?" Amory argued. "A lot of kids were dressed like ghosts last night, even Lucy and her Stone Age Girls, so why does old man Butler pick on me?" Amory paused, but Father continued to glare. "People just blame me because they know you'll pay the bill," Amory went on. "And maybe, maybe, I might be innocent. Did you ever think of that?" He smiled his winning smile at Father and then at Mother.

"Are you sure it was Amory?" Mother asked. "He's really not strong enough to do all those things."

"Not strong?" Father was off again. "He's solid muscle from all those tons and tons he's eaten for the last twelve years. Waste of perfectly good food!" Father complained.

The phone rang, and Amory jumped up to answer it. "It's for you, Mother," he said, handing her the receiver, while he whispered loudly, "It's Mrs. Flint, boiling about something."

Lucy couldn't hear Mrs. Flint, only Mother's soothing replies: "Too bad. . . . I'm so sorry," and finally, "I'll see that he comes over right after school, and Jerry and Stan will be with him."

When Mother came back to the table, she was hopping mad. "No excuses, Amory. Your ghost outfit was torn by the time you got to Flints', and she looked out on your red hair when you rubbed soap all over her windows. And worse than that, you boys printed CAVE MEN WERE HERE on every single pane of glass, so of course she knew where to phone."

"That was Stan's idea, not mine," Amory explained.

"Boy Scouts! So polite and doing one good turn after another," Lucy jeered. "Especially turning over outhouses!"

"You close your trap, Roaring Boring, or I'll put you on the stable roof next Halloween," Amory threatened at the top of his lungs.

By now Father was over the worst of his anger. "You boys wash all Mrs. Flint's windows after school. I've paid for mending the stable roof and repairing the Butlers' outhouse. And from now on you are all Boy Scouts and not Cave Men. Get the idea?" Then to Mother he said, "Halloween does excuse a lot. Did I ever tell you about when I was a boy and—"

"Stop right there, Harry," Mother said severely. "Amory knows enough!"

From Now
Until
Christmas

❧

That afternoon, Lucy was surprised when Hilda met
her at the school door. "November first's a special
holy day for us Catholics, you know," Hilda said.
"So I went to early mass, and see, Lucy, what I found
by the priest's corner." She handed Lucy a piece of
her locket chain—only a couple of inches of the thin
gold chain and no locket on it. "It is yours, isn't it?"
Hilda asked.

"It's mine, all right, but wasn't the locket anywhere
near it? And the rest of the chain? Oh, Hilda, I've
lost every one of my three gold gifts," Lucy moaned.

Then the bell rang, and all she had time to say was,
"Wait for me after school and show me where to
look—please do, Hilda. I'd forgotten that I wore my
locket last night."

Shortly after 4:00, Hilda and all three Owens and Lucy began to scour every inch of the board sidewalk beside the priest's house. But no gold glittered. The boards were old and splintery, the nails were rusty, and the ground beside the walk was hard and weedy. Finally the girls gave up. Slowly Lucy went into her yard, thinking of excuses to give Mother for having lost her gold locket on Halloween.

Inside the kitchen she forgot excuses and chain and locket. Mother was sitting by the range, holding Topsy, with sweaters around the little dog so that only the tip of her nose showed.

"Topsy was whining out loud. Now that I've picked her up, she's stopped whining, but look at her shudder. She must have a chill. I do hope she's not sick," Mother explained, as she lifted a sweater enough for Lucy to see Topsy's face.

Topsy's eyes were half-closed, very wet, and her ears did not perk up as they always did to welcome Lucy. Under the sweater, Lucy could see the dog trying to wag her tail, but the trembling and the shaking were so great that the wagging tail was only one more quiver.

"What can we do? Oh, what can we do?" Lucy repeated. Then a fearful thought came to her. "You don't think Topsy has distemper, do you? That couldn't happen, could it?"

"Klebers' dogs were perfectly well—so well that they were still sleeping in the cold barn. And Topsy hasn't been out of the yard since she came home," Mother comforted her. "No, it must be only a heavy cold."

"What's the cure for a dog cold?" Lucy asked.

"We'll keep her wrapped warmly here in her basket bed, and your father won't mind getting up in the night to put extra coal on the range so she'll have a cozy kitchen. Now you hold her while I get supper. She'll be happiest in your lap," and Mother handed over the bundle of sweaters with the shaking little dog.

At suppertime Father tried to comfort Lucy, but she could tell that he was worried. Topsy's breath now came in wheezes. "I'll phone the Langdon vet tomorrow, Lucy, to see what he advises. Meantime we'll just keep her warm—and happy, if we can," he said, as he bent down to feel Topsy's hot, dry nose.

All the next day at school—upstairs and down— Lucy's mind was on Topsy. She was supposed to drill the third-graders on their number cards while Miss Baxter worked with the two younger grades. But Lucy's wits weren't there, and Johnnie Kane scattered thumbtacks, Sammie Butler stole Trudy Meizner's collection of gold stars, and Liz Scheler stuck chewing gum in Dorrie's hair—and the whole room exploded. She went back upstairs, misspelled three words in a quiz, and forgot the products of Peru.

At noon Father reported that the vet said only, "Wait and see." And by now they could see that Topsy grew worse instead of better. Lucy came home in the afternoon looking so forlorn that Mother said, "She's best just lying in her bed, and you need fresh air. Run to Lowensteins' store for a can of salmon, please."

The errand took longer than Lucy expected, and it was early twilight before she started home. Passing the priest's house, she heard a faint squawk at the side of the road. Going closer, she saw Mirskys' huge tom-cat shaking something black. It was Magic.

"Stop! Stop!" Lucy screamed in her piercing loudest voice. The tomcat dropped Magic and ran. Lucy looked down at the twitching bird for one second. Then she snatched up Magic and ran through the gate.

"Father Van Mert, Mirskys' cat was killing Magic," she yelled.

The back door opened, and Father Van Mert lifted the limp bird, saying softly, "Poor crow, you'll need all your magic to get well this time." Then he said to Lucy, "Could you hold him while I see if anything's broken? It's going to hurt him, but could you do it?"

"I'll try," Lucy said. "I held my brother's leg when it hurt him, but then—he doesn't have feathers."

"Doesn't have feathers?" Father Van Mert inquired. Then he gave all his attention to examining Magic, while Lucy held the big black bird, feathers and all.

Suddenly Magic opened his eyes wide and croaked, "Stop! Stop!" Father Van Mert was so startled that he jumped back, and Lucy almost dropped the bird.

Then she remembered. "That's what I screamed at the tomcat. Magic has finally learned a new word."

"Hard way to learn a new word," the priest said, taking Magic and putting him in his big box-cage. "I'm glad he seems all right," he went on. "He's an odd pet, but you get attached to whatever pet you have."

"I know," Lucy agreed. "Today my dog's very sick, and I feel awful."

"I'm sorry about that," he said very soberly. "Tomorrow I'll want news of your pet, and you'll want news of mine. Why don't you come to call?"

Then Magic spoke his second new word. "Call!"

"Why Magic, you're getting very social." The priest laughed.

And as Lucy went out the gate, she heard Magic inviting her back, over and over again, "Call! Call! Call!"

Once back on the sidewalk, Lucy's mind was again on Topsy. "I can save an old bird I don't really like, but can I save my Topsy?" she said to herself.

In the night, Lucy was up three times with Father, trying to feed Topsy warm milk. But nothing helped. By noon of the next day, Topsy could barely breathe. Lucy and Father stood staring down at the pathetic little dog in her basket bed.

"I must tell you, Lucy, that the vet does think it's distemper," Father said very seriously.

"She's over a year old—not a puppy now. She will get well, won't she?" Lucy asked.

To this question, Lucy wanted a straight answer, and Father gave it. "The vet says a new inoculation is being perfected for distemper, but at present—"

For a moment Father hesitated, so all Lucy heard was the hard breathing of her Topsy. "At present—what, Father?" she asked.

"She hasn't a chance, Lucy." He stooped to put his hand on the dog's chest. "I've brought home the only medicine that will stop her painful breathing. I don't want to do it, but she's a sick, sick dog. I've got to put her to sleep, permanently." Father looked about to weep himself.

Lucy leaned close and saw that poor Topsy was not really like the dog she'd known, but shrunken and hurting. "All right," Lucy said in a steady voice. "But do it this afternoon while I'm in school." She seemed to have used up all the tears she had for Topsy. And as she ran her hand along the rough, unkempt fur, Topsy opened her eyes but didn't know her.

Though Lucy knew when she came home that Father must have buried Topsy and burned the basket bed so that no distemper germs would be a danger to other dogs, she didn't ask any questions. Mother was rocking in her favorite chair in the living room. "Come in here, Lucy dear," she called. "It's time I told you a secret."

Immediately Lucy thought of the secret that was hard to hide—but this wasn't yet Christmas, so it must be something else. Mother began by saying, "Ordinarily we'd get you another dog right away."

"I don't want another dog—ever!" Lucy said.

"Well, for the coming months we won't get you one," Mother continued, "because I'm going to have a baby."

"You're going to have a baby!" Lucy exclaimed. "Aren't you too old for that? I put forty-two candles on that birthday cake for you and I don't see—"

Mother interrupted. "Well, a baby we are going to have—at the end of February or early in March. I was going to tell you soon, since I didn't want somebody else to remark on it and have you learn it that way—I am getting bigger. But today you've lost so much that I decided—"

Lucy now broke in. "Mother, that's what I've always wanted, and of course it will be a little sister, and is that why you've been lying down more than you stood up? Now I can tell you that on my birthday I heard Father say he wanted the secret kept until Christmas and you said, 'Some secrets are hard to hide.' "

"Yes, and it grows harder to hide all the time," Mother said, laughing. "But I must warn you, Lucy, that we can't be sure of my having this baby until the first seven months of my pregnancy are over— and that's not until Christmas."

"Oh, I don't mind waiting from now until Christmas, and after that we'll be sure! And what'll we name her? And the northern lights might still be at their brightest and so she—"

"Here comes your father, home early. We'd better feed him and Amory and not live entirely in the future," Mother said, going into the kitchen to start supper.

Lucy followed her. There the sight of Father and the empty bed space behind the range brought back the memory of Topsy. "I can see your mother's told you our news," Father said cheerfully. But he saw Lucy's lips quiver, and he took her in by the living-room stove.

"There's not much I can say, but your Topsy was a kind of miracle to you, and in that you were lucky, Lucy. Not everyone has a miracle in her life. By-and-by you'll remember only how much Topsy loved you and how bright she was and how many good days you had together, and you'll forget the sadness."

And thinking everything over that night before she fell asleep, Lucy saw that this was partly right and true—and partly wrong and not true.

But Mother's having a baby was true, or would be true if all went well from now until Christmas. So Lucy lulled herself to sleep by saying softly, "From now until Christmas, from now until Christmas."

Only Men Can Vote

~ ✦ ~

When Lucy dressed in the morning, she remembered that she'd not confessed the loss of her locket, and she'd never told Mother about the lost or stolen thimble either. So as soon as Father and Amory were out of the house, she got both these losses off her chest at once.

She half-expected Mother to be cross or at least unhappy about them, but all Mother said was, "It's too bad that they're gone, but *things* aren't important compared to what you lost yesterday. I wish I could have spared you that." Then she changed her tone.

"Now this morning the Owens are busy, you told me, so why not go over and ask Hilda if she can come here? You've not seen Charlie lately either." Lucy recognized this as a scheme to cheer her up, but off she went to Dickermans'.

Hilda came to the door, holding Charlie in her arms and saying "Shhhh, shhhh" as she rocked him to and fro. "Come on in, and did you ever see a baby grow so fast? And smart—he's so smart you wouldn't believe it!"

Somehow Hilda managed to say all this and at the same time hush Charlie to keep him quiet. "I'm minding the house and Charlie today because Ma's sick again, and Pa took the twins—"

"Oh, I hoped you could come over," Lucy broke in. "What's the matter with your mother?"

"She's going to have another—in the spring," Hilda announced calmly. "That's why I always have to come home right after school. I got to look after Charlie."

Lucy quickly digested the news. "Do you mean your mother's going to have another baby? Why she just had one."

"But Charlie's four months old now," Hilda said, and when Charlie began to cry, she shifted him against her shoulder. "I've got to fix his bottle. He bottles now, did you know that?" she said proudly. "Sorry I can't come," and she soothed Charlie and let Lucy out the back door.

When Lucy thought she'd surprise Mother with the Dickerman news, Mother smiled and said, "I thought as much. Having babies is easy for her—for me, it's harder. Don't get your hopes too high."

"We'll wait from now until Christmas, and this time we'll be lucky, Mother. I know we will!"

At supper Father announced, "The generator's working, and tonight the electricity for Main Street and Fischer's Hall will be switched on. I thought you children might like to come with me to see the lights turn on, at eight o'clock sharp."

"Stan and Jerry and I are going together," Amory replied.

"That makes the occasion official," Mother said, chuckling. "Lucy, you go with your father, stop by for the Owen girls, and later you can tell me all about it."

"Electric lights! Just like a city." Lucy dreamed aloud. "Pretty soon we can have an electric pump and an inside bathroom, like Aunt Effie's in Langdon."

Father stopped her dreaming. "It takes more than electricity for a bathroom. What do you think electricity is, anyway?"

"Mr. Grady's teaching us in science about electricity and generators, but I'll bet old Fothergill doesn't know what a generator is," Amory put in.

"I don't expect you to learn about generators, Lucy, but I sometimes wonder. When you spend so much time in the primary room, what are you learning upstairs in seventh grade?" Father asked.

"Well, we finished Columbus and we're into the colonies in history, and in arithmetic we spent all last week figuring how many rolls of wallpaper it would take to paper every room in a house when every paper has a different pattern to match and every one costs different and—and—Miss Fothergill never gets the same answers we do, so—"

Mother interrupted. "But you did wallpapering in the sixth grade."

"Mostly she teaches us what we had before. Some spelling's new, and some poems, of course. She's all for poems!"

"Hmmmmm," Father said. "After Christmas, we'd better beef up your education somehow. The school board is getting a bargain in your teaching the primary room for free, but before long you'll be going away to school. You should be learning something new."

"I've been thinking," Amory began. "Mr. Owen's got all those expensive trains. How about his ordering a fancy electric one for me, and then when we get the juice, I'll be ready? It would cost only about—"

"We'll have electric lights in the spring, and your mother will have an electric iron, and that's all," Father grumbled. "Do you think I'm made of money?"

"I'm glad for you at the election rally on Monday night, Harry," Mother said consolingly. "You can read your speech much better if the lights are bright in Fischer's Hall."

"That reminds me," Father said, "at Fischer's Hall on the Saturday night before Thanksgiving, there's a big Catholic supper, with a turkey raffle. I was one of the first to buy chances, so I got tickets with small numbers—10, 11, 12, and 13. You start us off by taking the 10, Caroline."

After Mother nodded, he asked Lucy, "As the second lady at the table, your turn's next. What'll it be?"

Here was a chance to try her second sight again. She closed her eyes tight and mumbled to herself, "11, 12, 13." Of course, this year 11 was her lucky number.

"I choose 11," she said aloud.

"And you, Amory?" Father asked.

"The 13. Everybody says a 13 is bad luck, but I'll show them it's good luck when it's mine," Amory boasted.

"I'll take the 12—a good even number," Father said, as he passed out the tickets. "Don't lose them—they cost me twenty-five cents apiece." He stood up and began giving orders. "Lucy, you clear the table; Amory, you set up the dishpan and begin to wash and—"

"But I told Jerry and Stan—"

"You'll wash those dishes," Father commanded. "And Lucy, after you phone the Owens, you wipe the glasses and put them away and—"

"Goodness, Harry," Mother interrupted, "you're a real housekeeper now, though you sound more like an army captain giving orders to his troops."

Later, at the Owens', they found all three girls dressed to go out in the frosty November night, and with them was Edward. Lucy had hoped this once he wouldn't be tagging along.

"Edward begged so hard to see the lights," Mrs. Owen explained to Father. They all set out for Main Street, Gwen and Gwin on either side of Lucy, and Guinevere and Edward holding onto Father's hands.

They had gone only half a block when Edward began to whine. "Mr. Johnston, my legs are tired, and when I'm tired, I like to have somebody carry me piggyback."

Father stopped. The older girls turned to see what would happen, and Guinevere stared up at Father. Lucy had always heard people say that Father understood boys. Now she was curious about how much he understood Edward.

Edward stood holding up his arms to be carried. Father stood glaring down at Edward. "Edward Albert Christian Owen," Father barked, "you walk to Main Street and back on your own two feet or I take you home this minute. Understand?"

And though Father might not understand Edward, Edward certainly understood Father. "I'm coming, and on my own two feet," Edward echoed, as all three Owen girls gazed at Father in amazement.

On Main Street, a crowd waited to see the lights go on. Father wasn't opening the bank because it might confuse the burglar alarm, but a big new bulb hung over the front door. All the other places on the street—the hotel, the livery stable, the pool hall, the butcher shop, Lowensteins' store, the new drugstore —every building left or rebuilt after last winter's fire was now ready for its lights.

As they stood by the bank, the priest came by and stopped to speak to Father about the war news. "The whole Eastern Front has collapsed, I hear. The Germans will be stronger than ever. It's truly a world war —all the world will soon be in it."

Then to Lucy he said, "You never came to call on Magic. He's still croaking his invitation. And how's your dog? Better, I hope?" He smiled at her, as though they shared interests.

Lucy opened her mouth to answer, but she couldn't speak. Her throat tightened, and she moved so that her face was toward the building. Gwin replied for her. "Topsy died yesterday."

"I'm sorry for you, Lucy. I wish I'd met your Topsy. A dog is a far better pet than a crow, even though I like my Magic."

Then Father took out his big gold pocket watch and held it low enough for the children to see. Slowly the tiny second hand ticked its way around the face to eight o'clock. On the street and inside the stores, whole strings of lights came on. Everyone yelled, on the sidewalk, at the doors, and in the wagons, all hitched ready to drive home. Main Street glowed!

"Lovely!" said Gwen.

"Makes Wales seem truly home," said Gwin. "We always had them where we lived before."

"But ir Canada, all the houses had lights, not just the stores," Guinevere reminded her. Lucy sometimes thought Guinnie had been ruined by that trip to her Great-aunt Maud's and the change of her name to Guinevere. She never used to be so superior.

"Now do I walk home?" Edward asked.

"Yes," Father replied. "Here comes Amory. You wouldn't want him to think you were a baby, would you?" Amory ran past them, toward home.

When Lucy and Father entered the kitchen, the house was very still. Mother was dozing in the living room, where Amory was already curled up in a big chair, reading. There was no barking, no yipping, no scratching of dog's claws on the linoleum. For Lucy, it was too quiet. She hurried up to bed.

On Monday the upstairs grades at school talked of nothing but the next day's election of a President. Even Miss Fothergill let them discuss in geography class how each state might vote. To keep politics polite, Miss Fothergill, after the states were finished, called on girls for their ideas. Julie Meizner began. "My pa says that Hughes will put America into the war. And who wants Americans blown to bits in Europe? Old Hughes is pro-English, that's what he is!"

"Yes, that's just what my pa says," Laura Mahoney agreed. "Wilson should get reelected, and he'll keep us out of the war. Who wants to fight for stupid old England, anyway? We Irish hate England!"

Lucy glanced at Gwen, who was pretending not to hear. And though Lucy hated getting into arguments in school, this once she had to speak up. "My father thinks everybody should vote for Hughes," she began, "because if America doesn't go to war, then the Germans will win and—"

"What's the matter with the Germans winning?" Karl Bohn shouted. "We got no business butting in. The Germans are the strongest. Smart people will vote for Wilson and keep out of the war."

"Only the dumbbells will vote for Hughes!" Tony Alper yelled.

"My pa's voting for Hughes, and he's not a dumbbell. It's your pa that's the dumbbell! And old Woodrow Wilson hasn't got the chance of an icicle in hell!"

Lenny Pearson finished his speech in a roar; and Miss Fothergill moaned, "Oh, good heavens! Oh, dear me! Oh, see how we lose our manners when we talk politics— Oh, my—oh, my—oh, my!" The door opened and in came Mr. Grady.

He didn't say a single word. He simply stood, fixing his stare on one boy after another, around the room. The class became absolutely silent. Then he gave a slight bow to Miss Fothergill, turned on his heel, and went out the door and back to his own room.

Miss Fothergill blinked, heaved a few more sighs, and said, "That's enough on geography. Open your reading books to that lovely poem by Tennyson about the little brook. The words are easy, but I want you to learn to read with expression."

Everyone in the seventh grade dragged out the reading book.

"Now Cyril, you begin with that beautiful line, 'I wind about and in and out, With here and there a blossom sailing.' And try for good expression." Miss Fothergill clasped her hands and leaned back in her chair.

"Yes, I'll try," said Cyril. But when he read the opening, he imitated a girl's voice, very high and squeaky. " 'I wind about and in and out,' " he piped. Everyone snickered.

"Cyril, is something wrong with your voice?" asked Miss Fothergill, quite seriously.

Lucy looked back at Gwen and lifted her eyebrows, meaning "How can a teacher be so dumb?"

"Poetry always makes me feel different," Cyril explained, and then squeaked out the line, "With here and there a blossom sailing." The laughter increased.

"You'd better sit down and save your voice, Cyril. Now Lenny, you go on from there," Miss Fothergill said.

Lenny put his voice very low, somewhere near his boot heels, and began to read, " 'I chatter, chatter as I flow—' "

Lucy looked at the clock, saw it was time for her to go to the primary room, waited for the end of a line, and slipped out the door. Miss Baxter was new at teaching, but she was already a lot better than Hortense Fothergill.

That night right after supper, they went as a family to the election rally at Fischer's Hall. It was crowded with men and women from miles around, though the women, of course, couldn't vote in the election, so they had come only for the excitement.

The first speeches were for county or state candidates. Then suddenly Mrs. Towne walked up the steps to the platform. Before anyone could stop her, she was standing at the speaker's pulpit, which Mr.

Schmidt had just left.

"I'm not on the program," Mrs. Towne said in her strong voice, "not by a long shot! But I want to speak for us women. I pay my taxes on my farm just like you men, and I should have the right to vote for whoever's going to spend my taxes. Kids in school learn our country began with people yelling, 'No taxation without representation!' I get taxed, and I can't vote for somebody to represent me, and 'taint fair."

Loud *shhhhes* came from all over the hall, and some men were mumbling, louder and louder. But no one stopped her. "Other places have women working to get the vote, and Wales should know what's going on. That's all." And she went down the steps and back to her seat on the aisle.

Then everybody began talking at once, the women as much as the men. "She's got no right to speak at a rally." "What's this country coming to!" "Brassy of her, wasn't it?" And Mr. Drumont yelled, "You'll never catch my wife voting—not if I catch her first!" Mrs. Drumont, right beside him, laughed as hard as anyone.

None of it fazed Mrs. Towne. Though Lucy knew that Mother didn't think it very ladylike to want the vote, this time Lucy couldn't help admiring Mrs. Towne. She wasn't afraid.

Then it was Father's turn to speak for Hughes, and Lucy thought he sounded splendid. His rumbling voice filled the hall, and he'd planned what he had to say so well that everyone clapped—even some Democrats—when he ended with, "America must come of age. We're greater now than Europe, and Europe needs us to save civilization."

Election day was a holiday. The men went to the

polls set up in the hall, and by evening the men began going to the station to get the telegraphed election news, though of course nothing was final.

In the afternoon, Lucy and the Owen girls had talked of the election, thinking it the proper thing to do on election day. "I like our way best," Guinevere said. "We have a king and a queen, and we don't elect them."

"It is simpler, don't you think? And nicer without all this arguing and getting mad," Gwen added.

"Yes, but the king and queen aren't really your choice," Lucy argued. "Here whoever rules us is the people's choice." It sounded very grand, but she could see that a king and queen were grander.

"What's your second sight say about who'll be President?" asked Gwin.

Lucy closed her eyes as she always did to be sure of a different sight from what was all around her. Then she opened them wide. "Hughes! Charles Evans Hughes will be the people's choice," she prophesied.

"I believe you," Gwen said quite seriously.

"Does it make you feel funny when you second-sight something? And were you always able to tell what would happen?" asked Guinevere.

"I was born under the spell, so I must have had it, but I didn't know I should use it until Mrs. Stewart told me." Then Lucy felt she should be truthful. "Not that it's always been right, you know. If it was really good, I should be able to see where my gold thimble and my gold locket are, shouldn't I?"

"Maybe your second-sighting will get better until you will see where they are," Gwin said. "You might see by a kind of magic."

"Sure—like Magic the crow!" Lucy laughed.

That night Lucy and Mother waited up for Father and Amory to come home from the station, where the news was coming in on the telegraph.

Father had stopped to buy a pint of vanilla ice cream at the drugstore. "Caroline," he called as he came in, "look what we bought to celebrate. Hughes is in—no question! California's the only state not complete, but what is counted there is for Hughes."

"He's so handsome. He'll make a good President, won't he?" Lucy said. "And he won't really make us go to war, will he?"

Father chuckled. "Now that's why I'm not sure about giving the vote to you women. Listen to my daughter—voting for a man because he's handsome!" He said nothing about the war.

So Lucy said no more about the new President that night. The next morning she left for school early, to have time to tease those Democrats who had been so sure about a second term for Woodrow Wilson.

Before she was in the schoolyard, Tony Alper yelled to her. "What did I tell you? Only the dumbbells voted for Hughes, and now Wilson's in!"

"Wilson! You're the dumbbell," Lucy shouted back. "It's Hughes who'll be our next President."

Gwen came up behind her. "He's right, Lucy. Papa is just back from Main Street, and California went for Wilson."

"Papa isn't clear about the Electoral College in your politics, but he says California's last 4,000 votes put Woodrow Wilson in again," Gwin went on. "Even Hughes was sure he was President."

"And Papa doesn't like this the least bit!" Guinevere piped. "Now America won't go to war to help England."

"And Lucy," Gwin broke in, "what about your second sight? And what about Hughes as the people's choice?"

To comfort Lucy, Gwen said, "Couldn't Hughes really be the people's choice, but not California's choice? Couldn't that confuse your second sight?"

"Maybe," Lucy admitted sadly. And she went into her schoolroom, knowing she'd have a miserable morning with all those gloating children whose fathers had said Wilson would win. How could both her second sight and her father be so wrong?

At noon, walking home from school with Gwen, Lucy vowed she'd not ever vote for a man President. "I'll vote when it's a woman," she said to Gwen. "A woman wouldn't disappoint me like that. What's wrong now is that only men can vote."

Amory Wins
the Turkey
Raffle

As Lucy went into the schoolroom, Miss Fothergill stopped her. "Lucy, I just heard that your dog died. I know how you feel, and I'll only say how sorry I am."

For Miss Fothergill that was a very brief and sensible speech. Lucy was thankful. She didn't want to talk about Topsy, and she certainly didn't want Topsy compared to that slobbering Mr. Guggums, but she liked Miss Fothergill better for having said something. She was human, after all.

The family was at the dinner table when Amory came in, shouting his usual, "What do you know?" That always meant he knew something they didn't. So they waited to hear what it was.

"That traveling motion-picture show that was in

Langdon is coming here on Saturday. Now we've got electricity, we're just as good as the big towns. And Saturday night it'll cost twenty-five cents, but in the afternoon it's just for kids and only ten cents and Jerry and Stan and I—"

"Come along to the table, Amory," Father boomed. "I've one hour at noon, and I can't wait until you've had a whole motion-picture show."

"Harry, do you think a show like that is good for children?" Mother asked. "I've heard that some of these new motion pictures are quite—well, not quite what children should see."

Before Father could answer, Amory did. "Oh, I've got to see this one. It's *The Birth of a Nation*, and it's all about the Civil War, and our grandfather fought in that, so we should learn—"

"All right, all right," Father interrupted. "You can go, but on one condition. You take Lucy with you." Amory groaned, but Father went on. "I'm sure the Owens won't risk their children at anything so immoral as a motion-picture show, so for once you can behave like a polite big brother and do your Boy Scout good turn for the day, too."

"Me take Roaring Boring to a show?" Amory howled. "She'll spoil the whole thing! And Lucy, I read in the Langdon paper that it's full of blood and battles and murders and corpses." As he rolled these horrors off his tongue, Amory was trying to scare her with his bug-eyed demon stare.

"You're just trying to make me stay home, but I'm going," Lucy stated.

"It's full of gory-gore," Amory continued to argue. "Those Civil War battles were awful!"

"Amory, it happens that Lucy and you have the

same grandfather, so if you have to see this show for his sake, so does she. On Saturday noon, I'll give you each a dime, and you two will go together." Father emphasized the last words.

So when Saturday came, they did set out together, but once they were away from the house, Amory ran so fast that Lucy was panting by the time they arrived at Fischer's Hall. There, dozens of farm and village children were jostling through the doorway, paying their dimes to the black-haired man behind the table inside the doorway and then scrambling to the rows of wooden chairs.

The shades were pulled down and the electric bulbs, dangling on long wires, were brightly lit. Lucy had to push her way to keep Amory in sight, as he darted through the crowd to reach the two seats Stan and Jerry had saved for them in the front row.

The scuffling, whistling, and shrieking were deafening. But for anyone used to recess at the Wales school, noise wasn't new. What was new was the curtain the traveling show had brought with them and strung across the front of the platform.

It was a bright-green curtain, and on it was painted an enormous woman's head. Her cheeks and her smiling lips were a vivid red, and her hat was even bigger than her face, a hat that was all brim and feathers and bows and flowers, in pink and purple and orange. Underneath it were the words: LADIES, PLEASE REMOVE YOUR HATS.

Lucy giggled, since there wasn't a lady or a hat in the audience. But the boys were stomping with their metal-edged boot heels in a noise contest and they wouldn't look at the curtain.

After a while that curtain was rolled up, and behind it was one that the boys did look at. It was bright yellow, and on it in huge black letters was the sign: DO NOT SPIT ON THE FLOOR. Beneath those words, in letters almost as large, was the warning: REMEMBER THE JOHNSTOWN FLOOD.

For a moment, Lucy left the w out of JOHNSTOWN and read it as JOHNSTON. Then she realized her mistake, and recalled the terrible flood, mentioned in a history book, and how hundreds had drowned, trapped in their houses. The Cave Men thought it so funny that they nearly rolled on the floor laughing. She laughed with them; but when she imagined all those people drowning in their beds, the joke didn't seem all that funny.

Then a woman, probably the wife of the man who owned the show, came to the piano in the front corner of the hall and began to pound out a march. All the children clapped and cheered, the spit-warning curtain was rolled up, and there behind it was a white cloth screen with a wide black margin.

After that Lucy was in a world of costumes, heroines, heroes, villains, soldiers, guns, killing, burning houses, swords, and of dying horses and dying people, all interspersed with frames that told what people were saying. And Amory was right—the Civil War battles were horrible.

The first time she saw a man shot and mangled and then a troop of cavalry ride over him, she shut her eyes. The piano banged on, the boys yelled, the girls let out long *Ohhhhs,* but Lucy sat with her eyes squeezed shut.

Finally, in one of the breaks while the reels were being changed, Amory noticed she was sitting with her eyes shut. "Open your eyes, Lucy. Nothing at all to see right now." She opened them, but she must still have looked scared, for even Amory took pity on her.

"Tell you what I'll do," he said. "You shut your eyes whenever there's something that scares you or turns your stomach over, and then when you can look again, I'll tell you." And he actually smiled at her. For once she liked both Amory and his smile.

So for the rest of the motion picture, Lucy saw only what Amory thought she wouldn't mind seeing, and the rest was a blank.

That night Mother asked, "How did you like it, Lucy? Amory has described every single scene, but you haven't said much."

"I forget a lot of it," Lucy lied, to cover the gaps, which were most of the show. "But some of the girls' costumes were lovely, and you should have seen the funny big hat on the curtain and you should have heard the woman play the piano—every single minute of the show, music right out of her head, too, because it was dark and she couldn't see any notes."

Father laughed. "You see, our Lucy isn't harmed by a motion-picture show. And how about it, Caroline, why don't you get a job playing the piano for these newfangled shows? You can play for hours, making up music. Might make a fortune!"

Mother's only answer was to make a face at him.

The next morning before Sunday school, Gwin cornered Lucy. "Was the show good? I wish Mama and Papa had let us go. Tell me every single thing that was in it."

"Shhhh. It's time for the opening prayer," Lucy whispered. And while she put her head down and pretended to pray, she was trying to remember all

Amory had told at the table the night before, so she could retell it as though her eyes had been open.

Early the following week Lucy learned that Miss Baxter had sprained her ankle. Tim Hoffer was driving her to and from school in his beautiful green sleigh; but once she was in her primary room, she couldn't move about. So Lucy was asked to spend more time than ever with the third-graders.

Sammie Butler started a spitball fight, and Lucy zeroed in on him. "Stop that, Sammie," she said sternly in a low voice. "What will become of you, if you act like that!"

"I don't care. I'm rich," he said, sticking out his tongue at her.

The idea of a Butler being rich made her smile. "Oh, I suppose you've got all of two pennies," she answered.

"Look what I got," Sammie said. And out of his pants pocket he pulled three one-dollar bills.

Lucy was amazed. "You didn't steal them, did you?" she asked under her breath.

Since the children around them had now begun to stare, Sammie swiftly stuffed the bills back in his pocket. "I caught my pa counting a stack of them in the night, so he gave me three—and it's a secret," he whispered.

Miss Baxter became aware of something unusual going on. "Need any help, Lucy?" she called from the front of the room.

But Sammie had quietly turned to his book, the other children were busy again, and Lucy—not knowing what to say—said nothing. She could not help wondering, however.

So that noon, after Amory had rushed back to school, Lucy asked Father about the Butler stack of bills. "Do you think the firebug could have been Mr. Butler?" she asked. "Everybody says that whoever set those fires got paid a lot of cash. He could have set a slow fire, and then run here so you'd see him."

"Where'd you get that crazy idea?" Father blustered.

"But couldn't he have done it?" Lucy repeated. "I remember he said—"

"All right, Lucy. Just keep this under your hat, but recently other people have seen some of that cash, too. Where it came from, no one knows. And no one saw him near the elevators, either."

"He might have set the fires," Lucy hammered away at her one idea. "So why isn't he arrested?"

"Listen to me," Father said. "The Butlers are moving to Canada, to northern Alberta, next month. They say it's to make a new start. Nobody can prove anything. The best thing is to let them go."

"But he might be a criminal!" Lucy said in a shocked tone.

"No, we can't say that. Nothing was ever proved about those fires. And you don't say things like that about people when there's no proof. And no gossiping among the children, either, Lucy," Father warned. "Now off you go to school," and he opened the door.

The night of the annual Catholic supper at Fischer's Hall, the six Owens and three of the Johnstons went together. Amory had said, "Too many girls! Can't I have my ticket and go with the boys?" Father handed it over, first reminding him not to eat too much and not to leave after dinner and go wandering around town.

"Don't worry," Amory said. "We're staying to see the numbers pulled out for the turkey raffle."

"I'll bet my 11 will win," Lucy said.

"Want to sell it for ten cents? Of course it's not worth anything—but do you?" he asked.

"Never! It's worth dollars!" Lucy boasted.

At Fischer's Hall, the electric light shone out the big windows, almost warming Lucy as she ran with the girls through the stinging cold to the heavy door, which swung to and fro and open and shut. The whole village and the whole countryside were there.

The hubbub inside was enough to split your ears, with grown-ups talking, children shouting, babies squalling, and the clatter of knives and forks on heavy plates, and the loud calls of the girls waiting on table. "More coffee, anyone? More turkey? More dressing? More turnips? More pie? More, more, more—"

First, Lucy saw the small kitchen, full of perspiring women in aprons, stirring huge kettles, dishing up mounds of mashed potatoes, plates of buns, bowls of jams and pickles, and great pitchers of coffee. In the hall itself, the tables went the length of the room, and on them was even more food than she'd seen in the kitchen.

"Nine places just empty here," called Mrs. Schneider. "Sit down, and we'll bring you everything."

"I want lots and lots of everything," Edward shouted, holding his knife and fork straight up and banging them on the table. Then he saw Father scowling at him, and he added, "If you please." Father smiled at him, Edward smiled back, and Mrs. Owen looked very proud of her polite little boy.

As she ate, Lucy looked around and saw all the special booths—aprons to sell and pincushions, potholders, baby dresses, and mittens; and in one corner the curtained fishpond. There you paid to hang a line over the curtain and someone hooked a present on it for you.

But what really took Lucy's eye was the turkey hanging above the table with the round glass bowl full of tickets. This was no ordinary turkey. To Lucy it seemed at least as large as an ostrich. It was dead, of course. Yet in spite of dangling upside down, the clawed feet, the gigantic feathers, the long neck, and the stupid head all gave it the look of a monster that wasn't entirely dead.

As soon as they left the table, she searched and found Amory. "I've decided to sell my 11 ticket for a dime after all. You want it?" she asked.

"I sure do—an 11 isn't really any good, but every chance is a chance," he said, taking the ticket and handing her a dime.

Relieved that there was no possibility of having to carry off that turkey, Lucy went to the fishpond with the girls.

"Second-sight it," Gwen whispered, as Lucy tossed her line over the curtain. "I got a tin whistle and Edward got a red hair ribbon, but Gwin got a little ring and Guinevere's is best of all—a vase, made in Japan."

So Lucy shut her eyes and second-sighted. "Something good that I'll love," she said to herself, and she reeled in the line. Tearing the paper off the little package, she found a yellow clay snake, part of the paint rubbed off and the tip of the tail missing.

"Is that what you wanted?" asked Edward. "Because I'd like it, if you'll trade for my hair ribbon."

The exchange was made, and Lucy saw it was a truly good silk ribbon, though she'd have to argue with Mother about wearing red on her red hair.

Father Van Mert now went to the raffle table. He first thanked all the women who had worked so hard to make the supper a success, and he thanked the men who had sold so many tickets and the children who had set the tables in the afternoon. He even thanked the "people of other faiths who have come to eat with us at our annual feast." Lucy liked that.

Then he explained about the raffle drawing, and invited Mrs. Schneider, who was president of their ladies' group, to reach in for the winning ticket. She came to the glass bowl, smoothing down the wrinkles on her dark-green dress, where her apron had been tied.

The priest blindfolded her, she quickly reached into the pile of tickets, caught one between her finger and thumb, and pulled it out. Father Van Mert removed her blindfold, and said, "Read the number loud, so we can all hear it."

Lucy held her breath. If it was 11, she'd be glad she didn't have to go up to get that feathered monster. At the same time, she suddenly wondered how she'd feel if Amory won on her 11. A turkey was money!

Mrs. Schneider stood a moment, then called very loudly, "The lucky number is 11!"

"Who has number 11?" Father Van Mert asked.

From the back of the hall came Amory, his face all freckles and grin. "It's mine! I knew that number would win!"

"He didn't know it at all," Lucy said bitterly to Gwen. But when she saw the priest reach up and take down the enormous bird and hand it to Amory, she felt very lucky indeed.

Everyone now gathered around Amory and his prize. "I never saw such a mountain of a bird," Mother said. "I couldn't get it in the oven, even if I did have a big enough roaster."

"Maybe the hotel would roast it for us," Lucy suggested. "Remember the big stove in that hotel kitchen where we ate on our trip?"

"Good idea!" Father looked admiringly at Lucy. "Amory and I'll take it right to the hotel now and ask Mrs. Moors."

"And who pays me for all that turkey meat?" Amory asked.

"I'll ask Mrs. Moors what the going rate is for a turkey that size, and after we've taken out the last fifty cents you owe Lucy on her gold coin, the rest of the cash can be yours." Then Father said almost crossly, "I never did see such a boy! It was Lucy's 11, so it was her luck that you bought for a dime. You do take the cake—no, this time it's the turkey that you take!" Father laughed, and all the folks around them laughed with him, even Lucy.

The Bewitched Taffy Pull

Thanksgiving was usually a day spent with the Johnston cousins in Langdon, but this year they only
talked on the phone. It was Cousin Len's tenth birthday, so Lucy asked to talk to him. Once on the line,
all she said was, "Happy Birthday! What did you
get?" And all Cousin Len answered was, "Plenty."
Lucy handed the receiver back to Father. Her part of
the conversation seemed complete.

After Thanksgiving, true winter set in. The days
were very short, the air was sharp and frigid, and
every snowbank had an icy crust. Once a week the
three Boy Scouts met with Father to practice rope
knots and to work for badges. The Stone Age Girls
made presents for everyone in both families, mostly
feather-stitched handkerchiefs, and initialed ones for

the men. For Mother, however, Lucy was buying a special present with the two dollars from Father Van Mert.

She and Amory spent hours over the catalogs, choosing their own presents. But when Father saw their lists, he had a fit. "Amory, can't you add?" he exploded. "Fifty-eight dollars and ninety-eight cents, plus postage! Who do you think you are—a Rockefeller? A room-size tent, a rifle, a fishing rod and two reels, four new games, and—" Father ran out of steam, but he kept on crossing off items until Amory had almost nothing left.

About Lucy's list, Father shook his head and asked Mother to check it. "A lot of unnecessary finery and a total that would choke an ox," he complained.

"A new winter coat isn't really finery; but Lucy, you've not outgrown your old one, so you'll have to wait. And Harry, if she wants a tam-o'-shanter instead of a hood that fastens under her chin—well, she may freeze her ears, but she is growing up."

At school each room had a task for the Christmas program, to be held at Fischer's Hall. Every pupil brought pennies to buy the town tree, and the whole township—village and farms—was paying for presents and candy.

Lucy helped Miss Baxter's children make chains of colored paper, tie red string on lumps on tinfoil, and push threaded needles through cranberries for tree decorations. But the needles were often pushed through everything except the cranberries. "These children don't seem ready for needles, do they?" Miss Baxter said. Lucy agreed, only she thought they were all too ready. Everybody had punctured everybody else at least once, and not by mistake, either.

Both the downstairs rooms were learning " 'Twas the Night Before Christmas," each child assigned one line so that no one was left out. Mrs. O'Neil's room was also rehearsing a play about Santa getting stuck in a chimney, and Mr. Grady had promised to be the stuck Santa. His classes were to put up the tree, decorate the hall, build the wood-and-cardboard chimney for Mrs. O'Neil's play, and Sarah Lowenstein was playing the piano for the carols, while the other girls would help Miss Fothergill's grades wrap the small presents and bag the candy.

The money collection was assigned to the seventh and eighth grades, but it turned out that the girls had to do the collecting. The boys were interested only in picking out the candy, after the money was in.

On Saturday morning about two weeks before the Christmas program, Lucy set out with her list, mostly one side of Main Street. She began with the hotel, and seeing Mrs. Moors go in the back door, Lucy quickly knocked there, to avoid the lobby full of men, usually strangers.

Mrs. Moors, a tiny woman with her glasses perched on the end of her nose, listened to Lucy's errand, went to the china teapot on the shelf over the wide stove, and took out a fifty-cent piece. "How's your mother these days?" she asked as she handed the coin to Lucy.

"She's being very careful, Mrs. Moors," Lucy answered, feeling rather grown up.

Next was the livery stable, where she was not supposed to go. But there she was lucky again, for George Henderson was just going in as she came by. He at once put his hand in his pocket and brought out five dimes for her.

Now she faced the butcher shop. She hadn't been there alone since the day of the pork chops. She first went close to the window and peered in. Ed, the butcher, was standing on a high stool, winding his clock with a large brass key. As soon as she pushed open the door, Lucy could hear him softly whistling. That sounded safe, so she entered the shop.

"Everybody says that's the only accurate clock in the whole village," she said in a loud voice to get his attention. Then she gave her little speech again. "I'm collecting money for candy and presents for the Christmas celebration at the hall."

He came down, went to his cash register, punched a button that rang a bell, and when the drawer came out noisily, he stopped whistling. He hadn't said a word, not even hello.

Now he put his hand into the drawer and smiled at Lucy. "Christmas! In Chicago every shop on our street was decorated till you could hardly see in the windows. We sold fat geese for roasting, suckling pigs, and great round hams baked with candied cherries and pineapple slices, and—" He stopped, looked down at the open cash register, and took out five heavy shining silver dollars and handed them to Lucy.

"Five dollars!" she gasped. "Oh, thank you! Nobody else in the whole township will give that much!"

"Yah, I've got no kids of my own, and it's Christmas. Will there be a tree with candles?" he asked.

"Yes, everything! What my brother calls 'the whole shebang.' And could you come? It's the Thursday night before Christmas, at seven o'clock, so the farm families won't be too late driving home, and the tree's going to be lovely." It was a long invitation, but he listened to the end.

"Maybe I will, I'll see, I'll see," and he clicked shut the drawer, climbed onto his stool, and began to whistle to himself again as he continued to wind his cuckoo clock.

Lucy was still marveling over those five silver dollars when she came to the doctor's office. She knocked twice, and when nobody answered, she remembered that Mrs. Carmer was away and wouldn't be home until nearly Christmas. "Probably he sleeps late," she told herself, but she also thought of something else. She'd heard Mother say, "He's likely to get into his bad habits again if his wife doesn't hurry back." So Lucy didn't knock a third time.

The only person on Lucy's list who lived on the other side of Main Street was Mrs. Bortz. By now Lucy was freezing cold, and she knew that Mrs. Bortz, back after weeks in the country with her sons' families, would invite her in. The house was warm as toast, and in the kitchen Mrs. Bortz had a roaring fire "for a hot, hot oven—baking my Christmas cookies," she explained.

"Wait, I get you a couple of quarters out of my handbag. Lucy, you pick out cookies to take home—fill up this brown paper bag. Christmas is for eating—oh, how we used to eat at Christmas in Germany!" Mrs. Bortz exclaimed. Then her face suddenly drooped. "Germany—so sad a Germany now—the war and the wounded and the dying and the dead," she said mournfully.

And as Lucy carefully chose from the wide table of cookies—cookies with red and green candy, cookies with curling scalloped edges, cookies with more butter, cream, and eggs than Mother used in a month of baking—Mrs. Bortz stood beside her, looking down on the dozens of cookies as though they didn't exist. "She's thinking of when she was a girl and lived in a mansion in Germany," Lucy said to herself, as she continued to pick up cookies that were too beautiful to eat, ever.

Her last call was at the priest's house, and when she was about to knock, he came out, holding a mop. He laughed at her surprised expression. "The bishop is finally sending me a housekeeper, so I'm cleaning Magic's part of the house, and then I must also do the outdoor shed he used in the fall."

From indoors Magic was croaking "Faa-ther! Faa-ther!"

"I have only small coins," Father Van Mert said, as he took from his pocket several nickels and dimes and began to count them into Lucy's hand. "Twenty, twenty-five, thirty-five."

As he said "Thirty-five," Magic cawed from the shed, "Stop! Stop! Stop!"

Lucy giggled. "Not a very generous bird, is he?"

The priest kept on counting until he had given her a dollar. Then he said, "An old miser of a bird, that's what he is."

"My father's bird book says that crows are real misers," Lucy said as she put the coins in her purse. "They steal bright things and hide them, just like thieves."

"Luckily, Magic hasn't so far been arrested for stealing, and since he's a priest's bird, he'd better behave, hadn't he?" Father Van Mert laughed, gave the mop a shake, and before he went in, he called, "You can't imagine how much I enjoy your stamps."

Later, Lucy, thinking over the morning, said to Mother, "Only a few weeks ago I'd have hated asking all those people for money. Now that I'm eleven, I'm not so shy—coming out of that fear-spell, I suppose." And Mother agreed.

While they were working at school on the town Christmas program, Lucy and the Owens were also planning the Sunday school pageant for Christmas Eve at the church. Always the Sunday school was small; but this year several children were down with whooping cough, and the school was smaller than ever.

"Never mind," Mother told the girls one afternoon as they sat around the living-room stove, munching brownies. "Every year I've arranged the pageant so that angels can be added or subtracted. You need only Mary and Joseph, a couple of shepherds, and three wise men, plus as many angels as we can muster."

"Will you be well enough to play the organ for it, Mother?" Lucy asked.

"I hope so," Mother replied. "Pageant voices are very straggly without music, and there's no one else in the church who can play. Otherwise, don't forget that you girls are completely in charge of this affair. Even your mother," she said to the Owen girls, "needs a rest from church affairs. Now how about a rehearsal here next Wednesday afternoon—exactly twelve days before Christmas?"

"Couldn't we have a taffy pull afterward?" Lucy suggested.

"Good! That will bring Stan, Amory, Joey Dahl, and the smaller boys like Morrie Flint." Mother paused, then she added regretfully, "It might even lure the Kane boys."

Rushing home on the wintry afternoon of the planned rehearsal, Lucy thought of the long wooden box of evergreens that her Uncle Albert had sent from Virginia. Perhaps she and Mother could open it and decorate the living room before anyone else came.

As she opened the outside storm door, she heard men's voices in the kitchen. In a moment she realized one voice was Father's deep bass. Father home at four o'clock in the afternoon? She swung open the door to the kitchen, and immediately she saw that the other man was Dr. Carmer. She stood, with the door open to the shed, staring at the two men.

"Come in, Lucy, and slam that door fast!" Father scolded. "Want to freeze us in our own house?"

Mother was nowhere in sight. Dr. Carmer was saying, "Lucky the down train is late. With Bill Bortz's team and sleigh we'll get to the station in no time. I'll go to Langdon with you both, and Dr. Stewart says there's a room vacant at Nurse Dagby's house, right next door to his."

"I wish it were a hospital," Father said gravely.

"Almost as good," Dr. Carmer answered. "Anyway it's the best we can do. She needs a hospital, but she can't go 150 miles."

"Are we all going?" Lucy asked in a scared voice. "What's wrong?"

Amory came in, banged the door, and yelled, "I got here ahead of everybody!" Then he saw Father and the doctor, and he echoed Lucy's question. "What's wrong?"

"We're taking Mother to Langdon, so she'll have a doctor and a nurse with her. She may be going to—"

"Going to lose the baby?" asked Lucy in a wail.

"Could be, but we hope not. The next few days will decide that. Both of you go into the living room and give her a kiss. She's all ready. Hold open the front doors while we help her out to the sleigh."

Mother smiled a good-bye to them, but she looked fainting white, as Father and Dr. Carmer half-carried her out the front door, the storm door, and the storm vestibule. Lucy and Amory huddled together by the open door, which they knew they should close, but they heard Father call, "Mrs. Sanderson will be over to cook for you." And they were gone, Bill Bortz almost racing his heavy team of dray horses.

Lucy followed Amory inside. Her fears for Mother and for the baby she so much wanted made her eyes fill with tears. Her worst fear was happening. But she had no time to think.

At the back door there was a tremendous hullabaloo, and Amory ran through the shed to let in Stan, Joey, Morrie, all four Owens, and the three Kane boys. "Here we are!" everyone shouted, charging into the kitchen, shedding mittens, caps, and coats as they came.

Gwen at once noticed Lucy's sad face. "Did something happen?" she asked.

"They've taken Mother on the train to Langdon. She's very sick," Lucy explained sadly.

"She'll be all right," Gwen comforted her and put her arm around Lucy.

"Tough luck at Christmas," Stan said.

"We can rehearse anyway, can't we?" asked Gwin.

"C-c-c-carols p-p-p-perhaps?" asked Joey, whose stutter disappeared whenever he sang, so of course he loved to sing.

Then Mrs. Flint knocked on the front door and came in, holding Dorrie by the hand. "My little precious Dorrie is such an itty-bitty baby to come to a rehearsal alone that I brought her over," Mrs. Flint said. "I thought it would be so darling if Dorrie could have the leading part—be Mary, you know."

"I don't think so," Lucy answered. "She's very small for the mother of the baby Jesus. She'll have to be an angel." Lucy sounded bossy, but she'd learned that if you talked definitely to Mrs. Flint, she listened.

"Maybe you would like to be an angel, wouldn't you, honey-love?" Mrs. Flint said to the frowning Dorrie, kissed her, and left.

Only one part was easy to decide. Joey Dahl must be Joseph, since he was the only boy tall enough to be the father of the baby Jesus. Amory and Stan could be two of the three kings, but before anyone could choose a third one, Edward began to pout. "I won't be a dirty old shepherd. I got to be a rich king, bringing presents."

As soon as Johnnie Kane heard the words *rich* and *presents*, he insisted, "If Edward's a rich king, I'll be one, too."

By now Amory and Stan were whispering, and Amory sweetly smiled, often a danger signal with Amory. "Stan and I'll be shepherds," he offered. "We'll carry long shepherd's crooks, won't we? The kind they hook the sheep with?"

Before Lucy could warn the girls about the probable use those two shepherds would make of their crooks, Gwin said, "Splendid! Then Morrie can be the third king—all the same size."

"And the angels will be me and Lester and Howard Kane and—"

Dorrie interrupted Guinevere with a yell. "And me! Don't you forget I'm an angel!"

"Gwin, you'll be Mary, unless the Granger girls can come in from the country. One of them could be

Mary and the other could be the angel that announces Mary's going to have a baby," Gwen completed the planning. She and Lucy had already decided that they'd have to manage the pageant from the back of the church and not be in it.

The girls now busily measured everyone for robes or capes or crowns, and someone suggested the angel wings could be cardboard with feathers pasted on.

Since no one could play the piano, they sang only a few words of each carol and then gave up.

"Let's open the crate of Christmas greens my uncle sent," Amory said. Within seconds he had pried up the top slats with the claws of a hammer. "Look! Right on top—mistletoe!" he said in disgust. "We don't want that!"

"Why not? It's pretty with those white berries," said Guinevere.

"Pretty!" snorted Amory. "It's a kissing trap!"

"A what?" asked Gwin.

"You hang it over a doorway," Lucy explained, "and then whoever stands under it gets kissed. Doesn't Canada have mistletoe?" Then she realized it might be that a Methodist minister's family didn't hang mistletoe.

Amory dug down deeper for holly and pine branches, but the girls whisked the mistletoe out of his sight and pinned it high on the curtains that hung at the living-room doorway.

The next idea was everybody's. The big kettle of stuff for the taffy was on the back of the stove, and it was time for the taffy pull.

They pushed the kettle forward over the hottest part of the range, got out the breadboard and floured it as Mother always did, someone stirred and stirred the sticky, shining candy, someone else filled the cup with cold water for testing, and someone else got out the crock of butter for greasing their hands for the pulling.

At first, so many spoonfuls of the hot taffy were dropped into the testing water that Lucy warned, "Watch it! We won't have any taffy left to pull."

Finally a spoonful turned to a soft lump in the cold water. They then waited for the mixture to cool enough to pour on the floured board. Next each of them cut off a handful of taffy and began to stretch it and pull it the length of a foot or two. They pulled and twisted and pushed it together again, but it was not like any taffy they'd ever pulled before.

It turned to glue in their hands. Everything they touched was coated with the sticky mess. As they pulled harder and harder, they perspired, they rubbed their faces, they grew discouraged, and they gave up thinking of it as taffy.

Amory threw a tiny lump of it at Stan, who returned the taffy—to Amory's hair. Amory howled and ran for the living room, but in the one moment he stood under the mistletoe, Gwin threw her arms around him and gave him a loud kiss. Amory's screech could have stopped a train.

Then everybody began racing through the dining room, the living room, pell-mell through the house, around and around again, all dripping strings of taffy. Gwen caught Stan and gave him a smacking kiss, Guinevere caught Johnnie Kane and kissed him just as he knocked her legs out from under her; and when Joey tripped and fell on top of them, Lucy landed her mistletoe kiss on his ear. Dorrie was next in line. Instead of kisses, she gave hard kicks, to both girls and boys. Swiftly the heap untangled.

The chase went on until they all sank exhausted on the kitchen floor, still making breathless threats. "If I ever get you!" "Just you wait!" "You Stone Age Girls—bunch of savages!" Dorrie's piercing scream cut through the threats. "I came to be an angel, and my best dress is all brown taffy!"

Someone knocked on the back door. Everyone hushed and sat quiet, even Dorrie. Lucy went to open the door, and there was Mrs. Sanderson.

"Why Lucy Johnston, what is that stuff on you? It looks sticky!" Mrs. Sanderson came through the shed and saw the rest of them. "What happened? What caused all this?" Mrs. Sanderson waved her arm toward the taffy-covered table, the taffy-streaked floor and clothes and faces.

Amory was the only one ready to answer. "You could say that taffy caused it, but the girls—" He glanced at Lucy, and she looked so pleading that he grinned at her and then went on. "Well, Mrs. Sanderson, it's probably my Uncle Albert's fault. He sent us mistletoe, and I've read of people bewitched by mistletoe—honest, I have."

All the children nodded in agreement, while Lucy smiled her widest smile at Amory. She was glad she had a brother who was an expert on excuses. More than that, she was glad she had Amory for her brother. She was beginning to like him. How strange!

Two
Celebrations

That evening after supper, Mrs. Sanderson explained that she had to spend the night at Bohns' to care for a new baby. "Your father thought you two would be fine here alone tonight. I'll be back to get your breakfast," she promised, as she and Stan left.

Lucy was so weary that she soon went up to bed, and in spite of her fears for Mother, fell sound asleep. Suddenly a scream woke her. She sat up in bed, shaking; and although the bedroom was cold, she was perspiring. Then the door at the foot of the stairs opened and Amory came running up to her room.

"Did you have a nightmare, Lucy? What a scream! I thought somebody'd killed you! Lie down under the covers, and I'll go down for the lamp." In no time he was back again. He put the lamp on her dresser, where it shed warm light over the whole room. Then he leaned over the bed and smoothed the blankets over her, where she huddled now, shivering.

"It wasn't just the dark, was it? If you tell a nightmare to somebody else, it can't come back, you know. What was it about?" This time only hearing Amory talk was a comfort.

"It was about Mother," she began. "There was a coffin in the living room and— Oh, Amory, do you think she'll die?" She watched his face.

"Of course she won't die." Amory spoke in his most reassuring voice, though his face was not as sure as his voice. "Tell you what I'll do. I've got this book I want to finish. I'll pull up this chair, and I'll wrap up in this extra blanket and I'll stay beside you and read until you aren't afraid any longer. Okay?"

For the second time that day he gave her the smile that he normally gave to everyone else. And for the second time that day Amory was good to her and she liked him, actually liked him.

Father phoned Mrs. Sanderson the next morning, and when she came away from the phone, she said, "Your mother is just the same—very sick, you know, very. So your father is staying in Langdon, at least until Saturday. I'll come over daily."

Lucy moped through the day. If Mother was so very sick, she might die. That was something she had a right to fear. Even Father was worried!

When he phoned on Friday night, Lucy answered. "Your mother's so much better that I'll be home on the train tomorrow. You and Amory meet me, and we'll talk then." The rest of his conversation was with Mrs. Sanderson. But Lucy didn't care. She felt like singing even in her off-key voice. Mother was better!

On Saturday Father stepped off the train, looking very weary, but he waved and smiled. When he was next to them, he kissed Lucy and put his hand on Amory's shoulder. "This morning your mother's so much better that Dr. Stewart is sure she'll be all right and she won't lose the baby. She'll be home in time for Christmas Eve," he said cheerfully. "Both of you been good and obeyed Mrs. Sanderson?" he asked.

"Of course," Amory answered. "We tried to finish the taffy that Mother had started and that didn't turn out too well, but"— Amory looked up and didn't bother to finish his story. Father was taking them rapidly along Main Street toward the bank, and his mind was already on business.

"Don't either of you hang around Main Street," he warned and disappeared into the bank.

Amory went off toward Jerry's and Lucy hurried to the parsonage to tell Father's good news and to work on the pageant. Mr. Owen expertly cut angel wings out of cardboard and carved two very long shepherd's crooks for Amory and Stan. Mrs. Owen carefully ripped the side of an old pillow to furnish angel feathers, and Lucy picked them up and pasted them as well as anyone. Big fears that really mattered, she decided, could make little fears seem silly.

The one pageant problem unsolved was the organ music, since Mother obviously couldn't pump the little church organ.

"It's so much like a piano—isn't there one of your mother's pupils who might play?" asked Mrs. Owen.

"Sarah Lowenstein is the only good one, and they're very strict about Jewish things, my folks say. Playing for a Christmas pageant in a Methodist church might not be—"

"You're right, Lucy. It would be a mistake even to ask her," Mrs. Owen said in her gentle voice.

At supper Lucy asked Father about it. "Hmm-mmm," Father said as he thought it over. "Since you girls are running the show, why not ask another girl to help? Now that your eleven-year enchantment is over, you aren't shy, are you?"

So Monday morning Lucy waylaid Sarah before school. "Sarah, I don't know what your folks might say, but my mother can't play for our Sunday school pageant on Christmas Eve, and I wondered—well, I wondered—" Then she finished abruptly, "Could you do it, Sarah?"

Sarah looked taken aback. "Me play for the Christmas pageant in the Methodist church?" she asked. "I'd like to, especially for your mother, but my folks —well, they're strict, you know."

Then Lucy had an inspiration. "But, Sarah, don't great musicians, even if they are Jewish, play church music for concerts? It's the same Christmas carols you're playing for the school program, and it's really a performance, a kind of concert."

"I'll ask them, and I'll say it that way," Sarah promised.

That afternoon Sarah came back to school, grinning. "Papa says it's all right, so Mama says so, too, but now Davy wants to come. Can he?" she asked.

"Of course he can." Lucy's enthusiasm ran away with her. "Would he like to be in it? We're awfully short of angels."

Sarah shook her head. "No, that wouldn't do," she said seriously. Then she laughed. "Davy's not naturally an angel anyway."

That week the primary room buzzed, squealed, and

shouted more than ever, and Miss Baxter was help-less. Everybody knew only the opening lines of " 'Twas the Night Before Christmas," and after they'd named Santa's reindeer, they were always stuck, some of them going back to " 'Twas the night before Christmas" all over again.

Lucy finally lined them up, made each child recite his own words when his turn came and then shut up. She felt like an army officer, but it worked. And when Tim Hoffer, who regularly called for Miss Baxter nowadays, came in as the last line was shouted, he ap-plauded. Everyone felt rewarded.

For two days in Miss Fothergill's room, they packed dozens of red net bags of hard candy, though so many pieces were snitched and sucked by the packers that it was a wonder any candy was left for the tree. Miss Fothergill herself had such a long trip to Oklahoma that she was leaving the afternoon before the program.

Home was very empty without Mother. Mrs. San-derson came each day to help, and every night Father phoned Langdon to find out how Mother was. On Wednesday she was moved to the house of the Lang-don cousins, and that night Mother herself answered the phone. But when Lucy took the phone to say hello, both Mother and Lucy cried instead of talking.

Father moved Lucy aside. "You're all right," he said to Mother. "There'll be a baby in a couple of months, and you two girls just weep! I've paid for a whole minute of sobs, and you've not said a single word!"

But Amory made up for it. He talked so much that Father jostled him away and said to Mother, "We'll be at the train to meet you Friday afternoon, and Amory can finish the news then," and he hung up.

Friday afternoon! Lucy began to count the hours. But first came Thursday and the school program. Only Mr. Grady's classes had been allowed to decorate the hall and the tree. So the excited children and their parents waited outside the door, wondering what everything would look like inside. Lucy heard Father say to Mr. Schneider, "Looks and feels like snow, doesn't it?" But packed into the crowd no one was very cold and certainly no one was thinking of weather.

Then the door was flung open, and everyone surged in. "The tree! The tree!" the children yelled. And it was a tree no one would ever forget, so tall that it went up to the rafters, so wide that it had to stand out into the hall away from its corner, and so brilliant with the flames of its dozens of colored, twisted wax candles that no electric lights could compete. The whole of Fischer's Hall was a magic world.

A great *Ohhhhhh!* came from the children, and the older folks just stood and stared happily. Lucy saw that not only parents were there, but Father Van Mert and Ed the butcher and one-eyed Harry Sloane were all there too. Then Sarah played, and everyone sang the Christmas carols.

But in a short time Mrs. Flint came up to Father and said, "Isn't that fourth green candle from the left tipping a little?" Dorrie was hanging onto her mother, looking frightened.

"Look there beside the tree, Mrs. Flint," Father said calmly. "Every store and office in the village has lent its fire extinguisher for this, and next to each one stands a man ready to use it." Dorrie looked up trustingly at Father, but Mrs. Flint still looked worried.

Once the candles were put out and the electric

lights came on, the program began. Lucy helped Miss Baxter with "The Night Before Christmas." It went off very well, but afterward Lucy realized that it was Tim Hoffer who had saved the act by coming backstage and controlling the Kane-Butler gang. That gave her a whole new idea, something her second sight had never suggested. Tim Hoffer and Miss Baxter liked each other very, very much.

The rest of the program was soon over. The only mishap was Mr. Grady getting stuck, longer than the play called for, in the cardboard chimney the boys had made. They had measured it before Mr. Grady was padded with pillows for a fat Santa. He was supposed to get stuck, but once he was in the chimney, he could go neither down nor up again. When the crowd saw what was happening to him, they began to clap and stomp and yell.

At last, with a big kick, Mr. Grady knocked the chimney apart, stepped out, bowed, and said, "Wales has such good cooks that even Santa grows too fat here!"

"Why, he's like Amory, he can talk his way out of trouble," Lucy said to Father.

Then the bags of candy were handed out, and last came the presents for all the children in the first four grades. In the midst of that grabbing and screeching, Lucy noticed that too often the girls' red paper covered a mechanical mouse while the boys' green paper held a celluloid doll. But they traded briskly and no one blamed Dr. Carmer, the smiling Santa Claus who kept on passing out red and green packages until every child had a gift.

Then the village celebration was over. It was late, and people quickly wrapped themselves and their children in layers of warm clothes, said "Merry Christmas!" and hurried out. Soon the hall was empty except for the Johnstons. Father had promised to see that everything was shipshape and then lock the door. "Come along, children," he called as he lit the lantern and slammed the door on the deserted hall, Amory and Lucy now close behind him. "It's taken us an hour to pick things up!"

Once outside, Lucy caught her breath sharply as the wind hit her. The snow was coming down so hard that it made the dark even darker, and the wind blew in great gusts.

"Lucy, take my hand," Father commanded. "Amory, you take my other hand. We'd better go along double-quick. It's a real snowstorm!" And he set off so fast that Lucy felt pulled along.

"It's not just a snowstorm! It's a humdinger of a

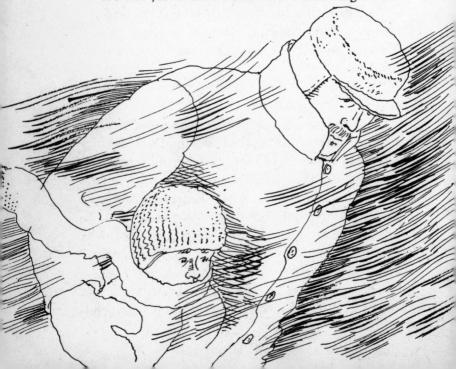

blizzard," Amory sang out. Lucy had no breath to say anything.

"The first block has no fences," Father said, "but if we get off the road here, we'll land in somebody's yard." Nobody said anything more on that block.

"Now we can see enough to cross this road." Father seemed to be talking to himself, but Lucy knew he was also trying to keep her from being afraid. For a moment he held the lantern high. "Here we go," he said, and across the road to the school corner they pushed their way against the powerful wind and the stinging snow.

"We've got a fence for this block. Rub your hand along it, Amory. It's on your side." In a few moments Father announced, "Here's our church—now across the road to the Kinsers' corner and then along the block to our back gate." And that's just what they

did. With Father leading the way, it seemed very simple. Yet only a few months before Lucy had nearly been lost, alone in a blizzard on this same route.

"Here we are—now through the open gate and along the walk—and glad I left a light burning in the kitchen to guide us home." Father kept up his talking until they were through the shed and into the kitchen. "Whew! This is an honest-to-goodness blizzard," he at last admitted. "If it keeps on this way, the train can't possibly get through tomorrow, and your mother can't get home. Lucy, what'll you cook for us?"

"But the train can bring her home the next day after that, can't it?" Lucy asked. "It has to—Sunday is Christmas Eve!"

"Now don't go back to your enchantment and those old worries and fears, Lucy. Everything will be all right," he comforted her. And she was so tired that she went right to bed, while Father banked the fires and Amory spread his hard candy on a tray to count the different kinds.

The next morning the wind whistled around the corners of the house and the snow seemed still to be piling up, though there wasn't a single peephole in the thick frost on the windows for anyone to see out. "We're snowbound," Father said cheerily. "Since your mother can't get home and I can't get to the bank, let's have a cozy day."

Amory came downstairs. "What's for my breakfast? I'm starved."

"You fix your own breakfast," Lucy growled.

"Don't snarl that way, Lucy," Father scolded. "You can be independent without sounding like a bad-tempered witch."

After Amory had eaten and they had all cleared up the kitchen together, Father suggested they get their tree in from the shed and set it up in the living room.

So for the rest of the morning the three of them decorated the tree, while the blizzard howled and the snow hissed against the windowpanes. They put the angel in her white satin dress at the tiptop of the tree, looped tinsel rope from branch to branch, hung glass balls, and carefully placed the candles in their tin clips so that no flame could possibly reach a twig or decoration. Next they put around the rest of the crate of greens.

"How about making paper chains?" Father said enthusiastically.

"No!" Lucy was very definite. "In the primary room I've had all the paper chains I ever want to see."

Some food was left from Mrs. Sanderson's cooking, so that was no problem. But the afternoon moved very slowly, all three reading books they'd read before.

By evening the storm had not slackened. Father kept trying to phone Langdon, but at suppertime their own telephone wire was down. Finally Father said, "Let's make the time go faster by memorizing poetry." And he began to read "Snowbound" aloud. "The snow had begun in the gloaming and busily all the night—"

"If you don't mind, Father," Lucy interrupted, "I've had enough poetry in Miss Fothergill's room, and I've had enough snow, too."

"Well, Amory, what are you reading?" Father asked.

"It's an article in your *Outlook* magazine. Tells all about men dying in the mud and ice in the trenches on the Western Front and how those things they call tanks aren't much good and how the zeppelins bomb cities."

"Enough!" Father barked at him, for Lucy was on the verge of tears. "Games? How about the three of us playing Parcheesi and checkers?" So they played one game after another, Amory always winning, and Father allowing Lucy to come in second. At bedtime they said goodnight to each other very glumly.

Saturday the blizzard was as bad as ever, though only Father stuck his head out the front door to check. So that day was much the same, except that now Lucy and Father got the meals.

"This could be a three-day storm," Father said unhappily. But by nightfall the wind died down, and Father stuck his head out once more to report. "Storm's nearly over! Just wait until tomorrow and see the job of shoveling we have," he said.

So Sunday morning was a shoveling morning, with Lucy working beside what Father called "us men," until by noon they had cut a path with cliffs of snow on either side.

Then Amory went with Father to the station to find out where the Wales train was and when it might come through. Lucy went to the parsonage. There they discussed whether or not to have the pageant that evening.

"A leftover Christmas pageant is worse than leftover toast. Let's have it, and somebody will come," Gwen decided.

Later Father came by for Lucy and told them that the snowplow was clearing the tracks down the line. The train was as far as Park River, and there was a chance that it might come through late that night.

"A train to Wales on Sunday?" Lucy asked in amazement.

"Only because we've been all these days without one," Father reminded her. "Your mother will get on the train in Langdon, if they're sure it won't get stuck in a snowbank between here and there."

"Mother home for Christmas!" Lucy shouted, and the girls joined in. Mr. Owen promised to go out and tell as many Methodists as he could that the pageant would be held at eight o'clock after all. Amory offered to alert the boys; and Father asked him to stop at Lowensteins' so Sarah would know.

By seven o'clock that evening the church was open, and Father had built a hot fire in the big stove, though the chill still nipped you a few feet away from it. To make the pageant seem bigger, Gwen was to be an extra shepherd, but when Stan caught her by the ankle with his crook, she decided to be a mature angel instead. This left Lucy in charge of everything at the back of the church—the angel wings and the kings' robes and crowns and gifts for the holy family, the shepherds and their crooks and Mary and Joseph and the doll for a baby. Gwen, in angel robes, carried the gilded star to the platform.

As everything moiled around her, Lucy wondered whether she could cope. Then Amory hooked a wise man-king and Stan looped his crook around Johnnie's neck, and Lucy had no time to wonder. "Amory Johnston," she ordered in a loud, threatening whisper, "shape up, or I'll give you what-for!"

Only about twenty grown-ups were there, but they all turned around to stare. Amory and Stan unhooked their crooks from the wise men, and Lucy suddenly felt proud of herself. Amory hadn't even argued.

Before Gwin took her place beside Joseph and the cradle-manger Mr. Owen had made, she gave a little speech. "We were going to have a much larger pageant, but the angel that does the announcing is out at her farm, snowed in. And a couple of other angels still have whooping cough, and a third shepherd is missing because he ate too much candy at the town tree, and—" From where Lucy stood she could see Father's cheeks puff out as they always did when he was trying to keep from laughing. Lucy hoped Gwin would finish before Father disgraced her, and Gwin did finish. "And Mrs. Johnston's stuck on the snowbound train, so Sarah Lowenstein's playing for our performance."

Mr. Owen didn't look too happy about a *performance* in his church, but Lucy was glad for Sarah. Davy was sitting beside Father, and now Davy would also call it a performance.

Gwin sat down and became Mary, wrapped in a pale-blue blanket and holding a baby doll, equally well wrapped. Joey Dahl stood beside her, wrapped in a dark-red blanket that Father said afterward made him look more like an Indian chief than Joseph, but Lucy thought he looked very dignified.

Sarah played "O Little Town of Bethlehem," and all four angels—Guinevere, Dorrie, and Lester and Howard Kane—came up the aisle, shedding feathers as they marched, but not singing a word. So Gwin stood up and pretending to sing to the baby, she led the music, and Joey joined in.

Next the two shepherds, their crooks swung over their shoulders, hurried up the aisle, and all the children sang "While Shepherds Watched Their Flocks."

Since every carol had several verses, all this took a

long time, and Lucy found it difficult to restrain the three kings, who wanted to be in the limelight. When they did go forward, with everyone singing "We Three Kings of Orient Are," they meekly placed their gifts around the manger. Johnnie's was a stick of incense in a holder, Edward's an open box of his prized glass marbles, and Morrie's a bottle of his mother's perfume.

Then all the children formed a line at the front of the church, Sarah pumped out the chords for the last carol, and everyone—grown-ups and children—bellowed "O, Come All Ye Faithful." Lucy could hear Father's shouted bass above all the others, but to her it sounded triumphant and happy. By themselves, she and the girls had managed the Christmas pageant, and it had gone off without a hitch. Mother couldn't have managed it better.

The
Snowbound
Train

~~~ ✌ ~~~

As the last verse of the last carol began, the four small angels scooted down the aisle; the angel Gwen sedately followed with the gilded star. All five pairs of angel wings scattered pillow feathers until that part of the floor was white. Lucy was relieved. Dorrie's part was done, without a tantrum.

The two shepherds stepped along, grinning and waving their crooks in time to the music. The three kings should have been next, but they instead went back to collect the presents they had left. So Joey and Gwin joined the procession, both complacently admiring their blanketed baby doll.

The wise men-kings, fearful of being left behind, now sprinted down the two platform steps. Morrie stumbled—Lucy caught her breath—but he held the perfume bottle high and it didn't smash. "Lucky night for the Flints," Lucy whispered to Gwen.

But the other kings weren't so lucky. Edward dropped his whole box of glass marbles. They rolled all over the church, with Edward immediately abandoning his fellow kings to crawl under the pews in search of marbles.

Only an Amory or a Johnnie Kane would have brought a match to light the incense, so of course, Johnnie had one. On the last strains of the carol, he came down the aisle, his incense smoking and smelling as though all the Methodists wanted a Catholic mass. Mr. Owen jumped to his feet, pronounced a hasty benediction, and quickly went over to blow out Johnnie's incense. The pageant was finished.

But for Lucy there was one more surprise. Stan came up to her and sheepishly said, "I'm sorry." Then he smiled—really smiled at her. "It was a good pageant, and we wouldn't have spoiled it. We were just horsing around, weren't we, Amory?"

Amory nodded and said, "Best Christmas Eve pageant yet—never had incense before. That was great!"

Father and the girls took Sarah and Davy to the door, since they wanted to leave at once. "Thank you! Thank you!" and "Goodnight!" they all called to each other. And afterward, Father said, "I wonder what Sarah and Davy will think of a Methodist service—feathers and marbles and incense. Such goings-on! A performance, all right!"

Mrs. Reynolds said to Lucy, "You laid down the law to those boys, didn't you? I never thought you had the courage." Father beamed.

Soon everyone had left except the Owens and the Johnstons. Father gave an extra tug to Lucy's scarf to be sure it was high around her face, and to Amory he said, "Button that top button. It's more than thirty below already." Mr. Owen blew out the kerosene lights, they stepped into the bitter cold night, and he slammed the door and locked it.

Together they went the few steps to the parsonage gate, called "Merry Christmas" and "See you tomorrow," and the Owens hurried in, while Father took Lucy's hand and Amory ran ahead toward Main Street and the railroad station.

The snow was so cold that every step squeaked, and Lucy nuzzled her nose deep into her scarf so the freezing air wouldn't be so cutting when she breathed. Looking ahead, she saw faint northern lights, low in the sky.

Father saw that she was watching the sky. "Your lights aren't much right now, are they?" he said.

"No, but I'm not so afraid as I used to be, am I?" she asked, thinking of Mrs. Reynolds' compliment.

"My daughter is cured of her spell. Abracadabra! Abracadabra! Hereafter she'll always be brave!" Father sang out in a loud voice. What would people think if they heard him, Lucy wondered. But no one else was in sight, until they turned the priest's corner and saw the lights on Main Street.

Every store had lights on, though only the Lowensteins' General Store was open—not for shopping, but for people to pick up things ordered before the storm. Men were going into the pool hall by twos and threes, and in front of the livery stable stood a line of box-wagon sleighs. The horses were all inside the steamy stable.

Along the street, everyone was calling "Merry Christmas!" And from each mouth came a great cloud of vapor breath. Past the post office and the one-room telephone office—both dark tonight—Lucy and Father went on toward the station. Amory was already there and pushed the door open for them.

At once Lucy saw that the waiting room was crowded, and most of the crowd were Butlers. She had forgotten that they were leaving now for Canada, and by the look of it, they must have spent the storm days waiting at the station. Mr. Butler was talking to a group of men; Mrs. Butler was holding Noreen while she took down diapers and underwear that had been hung around the stove to dry, and Nora, Aggie, and Gracie were trying to keep the youngest boys from mischief. All over the station benches were brown paper packages bursting their strings and broken-down suitcases and worn-out satchels.

Father led Lucy up to Nora. "Mrs. Johnston comes on the train tonight, Nora. She'll be glad to have a chance to wish you luck."

Nora looked exhausted, her coat unbuttoned, her dress grimy, and her wool cap askew. But she gave them a wide smile. "I'll miss you folks, but I can hardly wait to go. Canada! It'll all be new," she said excitedly.

Lucy looked over at Noreen and said, "Noreen gets prettier all the time."

"Most babies only four months old you wouldn't dare take on a trip like this, but Noreen's strong. Finishes every bottle, and Ma says she's the strongest of all the Butler babies," Nora answered proudly. Then she had to make a dive toward Harry and Ned, who were trying to climb into the ticket window.

Mr. Hoffer and two younger Hoffer boys and Tim and Miss Baxter were all standing together. "Is Mary on this train, too?" asked Father.

"Sure is!" shouted the youngest Hoffer boy. "Coming home for the holidays and going to bake us all the pies we can eat."

"We missed her," Mr. Hoffer said almost grimly, "but she's already hired for a good-paying job next fall."

"And Miss Baxter can't get home for Christmas, so she's coming out to spend it with us—and to meet Mary, too," Tim Hoffer explained with a grin.

Off by themselves in one corner of the waiting room stood Mrs. O'Neil, Polly, and Mr. Grady. Polly's attention was all on the Butler boys' antics. Mrs. O'Neil and Mr. Grady were deep in a low-voiced conversation, looking only at each other. "Mrs. Stewart was certainly wrong about my having second sight," Lucy said to herself. "It's Mrs. O'Neil that he likes."

Mrs. O'Neil saw them and came forward. "Is Mrs. Johnston really coming home for Christmas?" she asked. And when Father nodded, she went on. "How wonderful! People need parents at Christmas—my own are on the train. Poor dears, they've traveled for days to get here."

"Can we drive all of you home?" Father suggested. "I've hired Bill Bortz to take us in his big sleigh and there's plenty of room."

"Thank you, but Mr. Grady has hired a sleigh just for us," she answered so happily that in a matter of moments Lucy had planned a June wedding and a wedding trip.

Polly interrupted with, "I'm staying up, and we're all going to midnight mass, aren't we, Mr. Grady?"

"Indeed we are," Mr. Grady nearly shouted.

Father Van Mert came in. "I've been looking for you," he said to Father. And as Lucy talked with Mrs. O'Neil and Polly, the priest and Father talked so quietly together that Lucy couldn't hear a word. But she did see Father Van Mert hand over a small box.

Then to Lucy he said, "Magic wanted to give you some small presents, so I put them in a box and your father will hang them on your tree. Have a Merry Christmas!"

He greeted Mrs. O'Neil and Mr. Grady and explained to them that he'd come to meet his housekeeper—"that is if the train arrives before it's time for me to begin midnight mass at the church. And now I must say good-bye to the Butlers," he said, moving off toward them.

The door swung open and Amory stuck his head in. "The snowplow just tooted at the crossing! Come on out and see!"

Everyone began buttoning coats, retying scarves, and pulling on mittens. Mr. Butler and all the Butler boys hurried out, but Nora waited until she'd handed her mother a bottle for Noreen before she ran out with the girls. The Butlers, of course, couldn't board the train until it had come back from Hannah, the end of the line.

After the stifling room, the cold was a shock, but no one minded. Lucy stepped to the edge of the platform and saw the snowplow pushing toward them, cutting a path through the drifts, tossing the snow in great bursts on either side of the track. The round searchlight was like an enormous monster's eye, lighting up each flake in a shower of snow.

"Watch out for the plow!" Tom Evans, the sta-

tion agent, yelled as the plow came abreast. Everyone
covered his head with his hands and turned toward
the station wall—everyone except Amory and the
boys. They stood as close to the track as they dared
and let the flare of snow spread over them.

The plow tooted twice and went on to clear the
track to Hannah. The boys were all walking snow-
men, delighted with their load of snow, though Lucy
couldn't see it as much of an achievement to get plas-
tered with snow in a Dakota winter.

Then they heard the train whistle at the crossing.
The Wales train had never before looked so important. Its searchlight streamed steady and golden yellow through the dark, and it came much faster than
the hardworking snowplow. As it passed the single
remaining elevator on the other side of the crossing,
Lucy wondered whether Mr. Butler had been the

firebug. Now she'd never know.

The engine clanked to a stop beside the platform and noisily sent out a burst of steam. The door of the passenger coach opened, and the conductor put down the little stool. The first one off was Mary Hoffer, all smiles and looking brand new, in a red woolly cap, a bright-red coat, and a long white scarf.

It seemed as though half the platform of people called, "Hello, Mary! Merry Christmas!" And before Mr. Hoffer could slowly make his way to her, her brothers had grabbed her bags and hugged her and Tim had introduced Miss Baxter.

Mary saw Lucy and Father standing near the station door, and before she went to the waiting sleigh, she called, "Mrs. Johnston's on the train and she's fine! Merry Christmas!"

No one recognized the heavy blond woman who

got off next, but Father Van Mert went up to her, and at once she began to talk—she talked all the way along the platform, past all the people, and she was still talking when she got into the sleigh that Father Van Mert had waiting for them.

"In one house the priest'll have a talking house-keeper and a talking crow," Lucy said to Father. "Poor Magic, his three words won't count for much now."

Dr. Carmer, in his black fur-lined coat with the big fur collar, came rapidly along the platform and arrived at the door of the coach just as Mrs. Carmer stepped out. At first Lucy saw only her shining furs and her hat to match; then with a start, Lucy realized that Mrs. Carmer was as handsome as the doctor and that they lived their own close life, set apart from the rest of Wales. They murmured a few greetings, but in no time they were walking together toward Main Street and the two blocks to their office-home.

Once Mother had answered a question about why Mrs. Carmer put up with the doctor's "problem." "She eloped with him, Lucy," Mother had said, "and she still loves him, and she says she'll stick by him—always."

When Mrs. O'Neil's mother and father got off, Polly ran to them and they hugged her before they lifted off their luggage. Polly's grandparents, Lucy decided, were exactly what grandparents should be—white-haired and loving.

Then the conductor went up one step and reached down Mother's black suitcase. Father and Amory and Lucy pushed through the crowd toward the train. The conductor stepped up to the coach vestibule, and Mother came down the steps, leaning on his arm.

"Merry Christmas, Caroline!" Father boomed. "Merry Christmas, Mother!" Lucy echoed, but it came out in a broken voice, not at all like Amory's tremendous shout, "Merry Christmas, Mother!"

Lucy and Amory took her bundles, Father took her one bag and led her toward Bill Bortz's sleigh. They had to go very slowly because so many people came up to welcome Mother home. When Nora stepped up, Mother stopped to say good-bye. "May all go well with you, Nora," Mother said, giving her a kiss. "Write us sometime, won't you?"

Mrs. Butler now came rushing out of the station with Noreen in a mound of blankets. "Mrs. Johnston, look at our beautiful baby," Mrs. Butler called. And when Mother did look, she proclaimed it the prettiest Butler baby she'd ever seen, and all the Butlers grinned and Nora looked delighted.

For only a second or two, Lucy thought of the hired man who had run away, but Nora seemed not to miss him, and certainly Noreen didn't either, with as much family as any baby needed.

Once in the sleigh, Father pulled the two heavy blankets over them, Bill Bortz snapped the reins, the harness bells jingled, and off they went.

"Look at my northern lights now!" Lucy exclaimed. "They're shining on the whole village!"

"They touch everything with a glory, don't they?" Mother said. "They make our ordinary prairie village look beautiful, like a fairy-tale town."

"And that, Lucy, may be the best kind of sight your spell can give you," said Father. "Not second sight, but always seeing what's beautiful in the ordinary."

The
Lucky Spell

At their house, Father helped Mother out of the sleigh, they wished Bill Bortz a Merry Christmas, and carrying Mother's things they went along the front path between the high banks of snow. Father unlocked the front door, and once she was inside, Mother paused and looked around her. She saw the greens decorating the piano and bookcase, the mistletoe pinned to the doorway curtain, the wreath hung up over the clock, and there in the corner stood the small Christmas tree, with angel and tinsel and candles. And underneath were the packages from Minnesota and Virginia.

For a moment she had a weepy look. Then she noticed two large buckets of water under the tree and she laughed. "I'll bet my Lucy fixed those buckets. No fires for her!"

Father helped her out of her coat. Lucy took her hat and scarf and woolen gloves to put away in the kitchen coat closet, and then Mother sat in her favorite rocker, while Amory pulled off her galoshes.

"Your mother must rest in the morning, Christmas or no," Father began to plan. "So I'm giving some of the presents tonight. And I'll light up the tree in honor of your mother. Upstairs, both of you children, and I'll call you when I'm ready."

In a few minutes he called Lucy and Amory down. There was the tree with every colored candle lit, and Mother watching each little flickering flame as though it might set the house afire any second.

Leaning against the wall, beside the tree, was Amory's present. A real rifle—the very one Lucy had seen weeks ago in the loft trunk. "Wahooo!" Amory whooped as he grabbed for it.

"Careful of the lighted tree!" Mother shrieked. But the tree stood firm, and the candles only wavered slightly as Amory pulled the rifle to him.

"I was going to wait until summer and give it for your birthday, Amory," Father explained. "But you'd have missed half your gopher-hunting season. Mind what I'm saying—don't ever load it in the house." Then he turned to Lucy. "Open this big box and be sure to look inside."

She pulled off the wrappings that covered a beautiful leather suitcase, with two brass locks and a pair of keys. And when she lifted the top, there was a handsome, shiny flashlight. She stood, amazed.

"You're growing up so fast, Lucy, that before long you'll be going away to school. So the suitcase is for the new life ahead of you." Then he chuckled. "The flashlight is for a girl who once had fears, even a fear of the dark."

Amory picked it up. "Wow! When do I get one?" but nobody was listening to him.

"Now Caroline, my present to you," and Father handed her a long box. "I had your sister Frances pick it out so it would be just right." From the box Mother took a beautiful soft robe of rosy brushed cloth.

"It's years since I had anything like this. It's lovely," Mother said, and then she quickly added, "Are you sure it didn't cost too much, Harry? With all those coming expenses—"

Lucy interrupted. "Mother, I've got something for you, too," she paused. "Well, it's not strictly for you. It's for that little sister I'll have." The box she handed Mother was very small. Mother opened it, and there was a pair of pink baby shoes. "The smallest size Lowenstein's had, Mother. I bought them with the stamp money I got from the priest."

Amory looked up from his rifle, stood up, and from his pants pocket he pulled out a wrinkled tissue-wrapped package, smaller than the pink-shoe box. "I know it's going to be a boy, so I got you this for a present." He watched as Mother undid it. Under the crumpled paper was a very tiny, shiny new water pistol.

Mother laughed until she had to take off her glasses to wipe her eyes. To Father she said, "Funny, but I hadn't seen anything clearly until now. We begin all over again, don't we? Pink shoes and a water pistol!"

"Lucy, you've admired only the candles on the tree," Father said. "See what the angel has around her neck."

Lucy gazed at the top of the tree. There around

the neck of the Christmas angel hung her gold locket. She was tongue-tied. "Look at this branch, too." Father pointed, laughing at her amazement, for there was her gold thimble. "And now on this lowest branch, Lucy—right next to the tree trunk. What do you see?" It was her five-dollar gold piece.

"Where'd you find them?" Lucy gasped.

"Father Van Mert found them when he cleaned out Magic's hideout in the toolshed. Our pictures were in the locket, so he knew the treasure trove must be yours. Magic had stolen and hidden them all. A priest's bird!" Father laughed. "But that's not all," Father continued. "Look at this," and he thrust a big flat parcel at her, already open.

He was the only one who knew the secret inside it, so they watched closely as Lucy pulled out a large photograph—the enlargement of the snap she had taken of her house.

"I opened it by mistake a few days ago at the bank, so I kept it for a surprise," Father gloated. "And read the letter, Lucy."

Lucy read aloud, " 'The Eastman Kodak Company awards you a prize enlargement for your picture of a typical example of American domestic architecture.' "

Lucy stared. Then she asked Mother, "Is our house really domestic architecture, do you think?"

"Let's just say I love it because it's home," Mother replied. "But the picture is better than the letter—it doesn't talk big. It simply is our house. Congratulations, Lucy. We'll frame the picture, and don't lose the letter."

"I'm going up to bed and take my gun," Amory announced, "but first I'll make myself some sandwiches."

"Harry, don't let that boy sleep with his rifle," Mother protested.

"It's not loaded, and I slept with my first gun," Father answered calmly.

So while Amory fed himself, they one by one blew out the candles and then they heard the silvery sound of harness bells on the road in front of the house. "Must be the Schneiders coming in for midnight mass," Mother said. "These sounds of Christmas almost weave a spell around us, don't they?"

Then she suddenly burst out, "Goodness' sake, I completely forgot what I have for you, Lucy." She rummaged in her handbag beside her and brought out a pale-blue envelope, which she handed to Lucy. "It's your Christmas for letters. This one's from Miss Ross."

"What's it say?" Lucy asked.

"Open it and see, dummy," said Amory, who was standing in the doorway, holding his rifle.

"Read it out loud," Father ordered, sounding as anxious as Lucy to know what Miss Ross had meant by the spell.

Lucy tore open the envelope, with its King George the Fifth stamp, and took out a Christmas card with a picture of mistletoe. At that Lucy made a face, but turning the card over, she read:

Dear Lucy Johnston,
I'm glad your hair is red.

Amory stopped sighting his gun at the Christmas tree ornaments. "She'd be gladder about mine—mine's redder."

Lucy raised her voice and drowned him out.

The Lucky Spell

My first answer must have been lost, so I send this to you by the Stewarts. My cousin Meg Stewart was wrong about your having second sight. That comes only when you're grown. But because you were born under the spell of the northern lights, all your life you'll be lucky. Have a Merry Christmas!

Janet Ross

Lucy fixed her eyes on Father. "I knew that second sight didn't work, but doesn't the spell have anything to do with curing my fears?"

"Of course it does," Father answered. "I wouldn't want you to trust your luck so much that you lost your common sense, but this much is true—if you believe you're lucky, you'll always be brave."

Before she replied, Lucy thought a moment. Then she said very soberly, "But I don't believe I'm lucky."

"Not lucky?" Father exploded. "Look around you, Lucy!"

And Lucy saw on the bookcase her prize-winning picture of their house at the Edge of Nowhere, and on the tree she saw her three golden gifts miraculously restored by Magic.

She saw Amory and Father, and then Mother in her rocking chair—Mother home for Christmas and not going to die. And in a couple of months there would be a baby.

Mother held out her arms, and Lucy ran to her. "I am lucky, I know I am," Lucy told her. "And my spell of the northern lights must be a lucky spell."